Paige doubted very much that Valentino understood the potential impact of this test. How could a footloose, fancy-free playboy bachelor understand the full implications? For him it was no doubt a test of his virility. Proof of his manliness... But for her? It was a whole different proposition.

Still, regardless of that, it did need to be done—so she took a deep breath. But even before the little plus appeared, somewhere inside she knew.

"Well?" Valentino asked as she came back into the open lounge area.

Paige held up the test, barely keeping upright as the foundations of her world crashed all around her. "It's positive."

Valentino stared at the pink plus sign. It was a full minute before the information sank in. He was going to be a father. He smiled. And then he grinned. "This is the best news ever."

Paige wasn't similarly overcome. In fact, a huge block of emotion built in her chest till she thought she was going to pass out from the pressure of it. It stung her eyes and prickled in her nose. She sucked in a breath. "No, Valentino, it's not. This is the worst possible news. You have no idea."

And she burst into tears.

Dear Reader,

What is it about Italian men? Is it their dark, brooding looks, their seemingly effortless charisma, or that accent? Why are they so popular in our books? Why do we love to read about them so much? I'm not sure I know the reason myself, but I'm sure my two heroines Nat and Paige do!

When my editor suggested I write two linked books with Italian heroes I didn't hesitate. I've had such fun writing them in the past, how could I resist? And what fabulous men my muse presented to me! Cousins Alessandro and Valentino Lombardi have so much in common—both specialist doctors, both compassionate and honorable men, growing up like brothers in Italy and forging new lives for themselves on the opposite side of the world. But also, in many ways, they are complete opposites.

Alessandro, so strained and serious, failing to cope with the death of his wife while raising his four-year-old son. And Valentino, the fun-loving, easygoing Lothario.

It seemed only right to give them women they needed. Or who needed them. Nat, so bright and peppy, and determined to forge a bond between Alessandro and his son. And Paige, single mother of a deaf child, so fragile and shut down—a combination that a hot-blooded Italian like Valentino finds hard to resist. I hope you enjoy their stories as these four special people find their way to love. I know I certainly enjoyed writing them.

I miss them already.

Love,

Amy

VALENTINO'S PREGNANCY BOMBSHELL
Amy Andrews

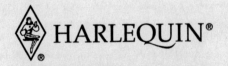

TORONTO • NEW YORK • LONDON
AMSTERDAM • PARIS • SYDNEY • HAMBURG
STOCKHOLM • ATHENS • TOKYO • MILAN • MADRID
PRAGUE • WARSAW • BUDAPEST • AUCKLAND

Recycling programs
for this product may
not exist in your area.

ISBN-13: 978-0-373-06755-8

VALENTINO'S PREGNANCY BOMBSHELL

First North American Publication 2010

Copyright © 2010 by Amy Andrews

For questions and comments about the quality of this book please contact us at Customer_eCare@Harlequin.ca.

www.eHarlequin.com

Printed in U.S.A.

ITALIAN SURGEON...TO DAD!

Welcome to Amy Andrews's enchanting new **Italian Surgeon...to Dad!** duet, introducing the two devastatingly gorgeous Lombardi surgeons.

Bubbly nanny Natalie has put the smile back on single dad Alessandro's little boy—but can she win over the brooding surgeon's heart?

ALESSANDRO AND THE CHEERY NANNY

Single mom Paige has her hands full with a young daughter who is hearing impaired. Now she must find the courage to tell playboy Valentino she's expecting his baby!

VALENTINO'S PREGNANCY BOMBSHELL

ITALIAN SURGEON...TO DAD!

On call for the hospital—and the nursery!

This book is dedicated to all those bionic ear pioneers who strove to give deaf people everywhere options they'd never had before.

Such achievements are totally inspiring.

CHAPTER ONE

PAIGE DONALD could feel Valentino Lombardi's gaze on her from across the altar. Not even the beauty of the ceremony or the happiness in her heart for her friend, Natalie, could distract her from the intensity of it.

It caressed every inch of her body, making her even more self-conscious about what she was wearing.

The bridesmaid's dress clung to non-existent curves. The hem grazed her knee and she suppressed the urge to yank it lower. This wasn't her. This frothy, clingy, femme fatale dress with shoestring straps and low back.

Very. Low. Back.

The crimson creation didn't say busy single working mother with a high-needs child who hasn't slept an entire night through in three years.

It said Sexy. Flirty. Time for pleasure. It said the playground is open, come on in. And Valentino Lombardi, possibly the sexiest man she'd ever laid eyes on, probably the sexiest man in existence, looked like he wanted to be first to ride.

But she didn't have time. Not for flirting. Or riding.

Or pleasure. Or any of those trivialities. And especially not for a man who looked like he held a PhD in trivia. There were never enough hours in the day as it was.

There was just never enough time.

She had a sudden hankering for her faded grey track-pants and her favourite oversized T-shirt back in her wardrobe at home in Brisbane. Or better still her baggy blue scrubs. She didn't like being this…on display. She felt awkward.

The heat from Valentino's gaze radiated towards her and she slid him a mutinous back-off-buddy glance. It was one she'd perfected since Arnie had walked out on her and it usually stopped a man dead in his tracks. But Valentino just grinned and gave her a saucy wink.

Great! Please, God, don't let me have to dodge this Italian Neanderthal all night.

'Can I have the rings, please?'

Paige could have kissed the priest as Alessandro's best man was given a job to do other than look at her. Unfortunately, though, his actions commanded the attention of the entire female population of the church, including her, and Paige found herself drinking in the way his exquisite suit pulled across broad shoulders and how the fine wool of his trousers outlined powerful quads and one very fine backside.

Very, very fine.

He glanced at her as he stepped back into his place and his espresso eyes told her he knew exactly where hers had been. A smile touched his lips, beautiful lips that could have been carved by one of the masters. Except they were warm and vital.

Desirable. Kissable.

There was a frankness in his gaze that stopped the breath in her lungs. She searched for something more, beyond the promise of tonight. Something deeper. A connection. Something that told her he was interested in more than getting her between his sheets. But all she found was heat and sex and lust.

Totally superficial. Like the man.

Another flashy male. All sparkle, no substance.

Still, her heart skipped a beat and she sucked in a ragged breath.

Paige hit the 'send' button and placed her mobile on the table, drumming her fingers. Her gaze returned, yet again, to Valentino as he worked the room. She tried to ignore him and her steadily growing irritation as women almost swooned at his feet but the rich sound of his easy, frequent laughter made it impossible. It reached out from across the room as if he had physically caressed her, drawing her attention like a moth to flame.

Valentino Lombardi was not a man you could ignore. With his killer dimples, boyishly curly hair and Italian playboy charm, he was pure vice.

Paige's phone vibrated and she reached for it, her pulse spiking.

McKenzie fine. Sleeping well. Stop worrying.

Paige's fingers flew over the keypad. *Apnoea mat on?*

Alessandro laughed again and Paige drank the sight of him in as she pressed 'send'. He threw his head back, giving the belly laugh its full freedom, and her gaze followed the bronzed length of his exposed neck peppered with dark stubble.

Another vibration dragged her eyes back to the table. *Yes. Go and dance for crying out loud!*

Paige smiled despite the gnawing, ever-present worry. She could almost hear her mother saying the words. But she'd never had a night away from her daughter. Frankly she didn't know what to do with herself.

Don't think I'll stay the night. If I leave after cake can be home by midnight. 'Send'.

Paige checked her watch, doing a quick calculation in her head. Yep. She could definitely make it home by then.

'Everything okay?'

Paige glanced up into the bride's face. Nat had fresh bluebells threaded into her blonde locks, which brought out the colour of her eyes and matched the crystal beading decorating the neckline of her ivory gown. Alessandro's hand rested possessively on her shoulder and Paige felt a sudden yearning she couldn't explain.

Why? She'd been where they were. Had the divorce to prove it. She certainly had no desire to do it again.

She smiled at her friend. 'Just telling Mum I might not stay the night.'

'Paige? No.' Nat grabbed her hand. 'Your parents have booked and paid for it. Including breakfast. Your mother would skin me alive if I let you leave.' Nat squeezed Paige's hand. 'It's just one night. Don't you think it's time you enjoyed a well-deserved break?'

Paige shied away from the earnestness of her friend's expression. Everyone said that to her—you need a break, Paige. But she was a mother first and foremost and McKenzie needed her. That's just the way it was. Nat would understand one day too.

The phone vibrated and Paige grabbed it, relieved to break eye contact with the bride. She opened the message and read it three times, a ghost of a smile touching her lips. She held it up to Nat.

Don't. You. Dare.

Nat grinned. 'Have I mentioned how much I like your mother?'

Paige rolled her eyes. 'Okay, okay. I'll stay.'

'Good.' Nat squeezed her hand. 'The speeches are about to start.'

A deep laugh floated towards them and Nat looked across to where Valentino was chatting with some nurses from their work. 'You should take a page out of Val's book. He's certainly having a good time.'

Paige felt her gaze drawing to him again. 'Isn't he just,' she said dryly.

Nat sighed. 'I tell you, if I wasn't utterly besotted with Alessandro and was up for a brief fling, I'd be over there too.'

'Hmm,' Paige murmured noncommittally.

'Do you know he used to date Adrianna de Luca?'

Paige gave her friend a mystified look. 'Who?'

Nat rolled her eyes. 'One of Italy's top catwalk models.'

Of course he did. 'Fancy that.'

'They were in all the magazines last year.'

Paige hadn't read a magazine in for ever. Or a book. Sunday newspapers were about her limit. 'Of course they were.' Her voice dripped with derision.

Nat regarded her friend seriously. 'Not all men are like Arnie, Paige.' She looked up as Valentino laughed again and poked her elbow into Paige's ribs. 'Come on, you have to admit, he's a bit of a spunk.'

'I hope you're talking about me, *il mio tesoro*,' Alessandro interrupted, nuzzling his new wife's neck.

'But of course.' Nat smiled, turning to Alessandro, her lips poised to meet his as he lowered his head.

Paige felt a tug at her dress and was grateful for a reason to avoid the blissful clinch she knew was happening beside her. She looked down to see, Juliano, Alessandro's four year old son.

'Where's McKenzie?'

Paige smiled at the boy. 'Juliano, you look magnificent!' He was dressed in a mini-tux and was the spitting image of his father.

With the boyishness and dimples of his father's cousin.

Juliano stood a little higher. 'Nat says I'm handsome.'

'Nat is one hundred per cent right.'

Juliano beamed. 'Is McKenzie sick?'

Paige shook her head, saddened that it was such a natural conclusion for Juliano to jump to. 'No. She's at home with her grandparents.'

Juliano's face fell. 'I wanted to ask her to dance.'

Paige's heart just about melted and she pulled Juliano in for a big hug. 'You are so sweet. I see you have your father's charm.' She glanced at Alessandro, who winked at her. 'Another time, huh?'

Nat had wanted McKenzie to be her flower girl but Paige had declined. The truth was, crowds made Paige very nervous for her daughter. As an ex-prem with chronic lung disease and poor immunity, every single person was a potential source of infection, a silver bullet to McKenzie's weak defences. It just wasn't worth the risk.

'Okay.' Juliano nodded, squirming out of her embrace. 'See ya,' he chirped, and ducked away, heading for the dance floor.

Paige watched him, smiling even though her heart ached. What would she give for her daughter to be so able-bodied, so carefree? She returned her attention to her phone and replied to her mother's text.

Promise you'll ring if there's a problem.

It took five seconds for the reply. *I promise.*

Paige texted back. *Anything at all. No matter how trivial.* She released the message into the ether and held on fast to the phone, tension tightening her stomach muscles.

She knew people thought she was too uptight about her daughter but what did they know? It was she who lived every day with the reality of McKenzie's fragile health, not them. And one thing was for certain—being vigilant had kept McKenzie alive.

With the operation only a couple of months away now, Paige was determined to keep McKenzie healthy and avoid any more delays. It had been rescheduled three times already. No more.

The phone vibrated in her hand and Paige opened the message. *I'm switching the phone off now. Go and have fun. That's an order.*

Paige smiled. She'd obviously stretched her mother's patience enough for one night. Thank God for her parents. She would never have got through the past few years without them.

A tinkling of cutlery on glass cut through the low murmur and Paige turned to see Alessandro standing. She pushed all thoughts of the world outside the room aside, determined to follow her mother's orders, and motioned for the drinks waiter.

'So,' Valentino said, topping up Paige's half-full glass with some more champagne, 'I believe it is a custom in your country for the best man and the bridesmaid to dance the bridal waltz together.'

His voice was low and close to her ear and her body reacted as if he had suggested something much more risqué than a customary dance in front of a room full of people. It took all her willpower not to melt into a puddle. Not to turn her head and flirt like crazy.

Except it seemed like a million years ago now that she'd last flirted and she was pretty sure she didn't have a clue how to go about it. And why she would choose to do so with a man who was all glamour and sparkle, after her experience with Arnie, was beyond her.

The bitter burn of memories was never far from reach.

'That's right,' she said, refusing to look at him, focusing instead on the bubbles meandering to the surface of her champagne.

'*Eccellente.* I'm looking forward to that.'

Well, that made one of them. The thought of them dancing, his arm around her practically bare back, their bodies close, was sending her heart into fibrillation. Sitting next to him at the table, aware of his every move, every breath, their arms occasionally brushing, his deep voice resonating through tense abdominal muscles, was bad enough. Being pressed along the magnificent tuxedoed length of him? Frankly it scared the hell out of her.

She felt gauche and unsophisticated and totally out of her depth next to his man-of-the-world, model-dating perfection.

What if she stuffed up the steps? Or trod on his foot?

What if she liked it too much?

'You are worried your boyfriend will mind that we dance, yes?'

Valentino's comment snapped her out of the vision of her clinging to him like some sort of groupie as he pressed kisses down her neck. She glanced at him, startled.

A big mistake.

Thus far she'd managed not to look at him this close up. And now she knew why. This near, he was simply dazzling. Gorgeous hair the colour of midnight waved in haphazard glory, thick and lustrous with not a hint of grey. It brushed his forehead and collar and Paige finally understood the itch some women talked about to run their fingers through a man's hair.

Jet-black eyebrows quirked at her as her gaze widened to take in his square jaw line, heavy with five-o'clock shadow. His full lips curved upward and were bracketed by dimples that should be outlawed on anyone over five. His eyes, dark like a shot of the best Italian espresso, were fringed by long black lashes and promised fun and flirting.

A buzz coursed through her veins at the fifteen different kinds of sin she could see in them.

Valentino smiled at the little frown that knitted Paige's caramel brows together and crinkled her forehead. She was a most intriguing woman. Her grey eyes were huge in her angular face dominated by prominent cheekbones and a wide mouth.

She wore no eye make-up to enhance them, she didn't need to. They drew the gaze regardless. Her strawberry-blonde hair had been severely styled into a pixie cut that feathered over her forehead and would have looked boyish on anyone else but only seemed to enhance the hugeness of her eyes and the vulnerability he saw there.

She was no beauty. She certainly wasn't his usual type. He liked them curvy. Everywhere. Not rail thin like Paige. And confident. Women who were secure in their sexuality, who smiled and flirted and enjoyed life. Women who knew the score.

And yet…

There was something about her that intrigued him. Not least of all the fact that she'd been the only female in the room who hadn't clamoured to be closer to him.

'I see you texting. All night,' he prompted when she still didn't say anything. 'I figure a beautiful woman…' He shrugged and shot her his best hey-baby grin, 'it must be a boyfriend?'

Paige shook her head to clear it as Valentino's smile muddled her senses. 'I'm a little old for a boyfriend, don't you think?'

'Paige. We are never too old for love.'

The slight reprimand in his voice didn't register. Nothing registered beyond the way he'd said her name. Paige. He had drawn it out a little at the end, giving it a very European flair, and it had stroked across every nerve ending in her pelvis.

She shut her eyes. This was madness. He was just a man. God knew, she hadn't even thought about the opposite sex since her husband had walked out on her. And, besides, she just didn't have time for a man. Especially not a model-dating, Italian playboy whose interest in her would no doubt wane the minute after he had his way with her.

Which wasn't going to happen.

Even if, deep down, in a secret, hidden part of her, she wanted it very, very badly.

I am a single-mother of a high-needs child.

I am a single mother of a high-needs child.

She turned back to her champagne and took a long deep swallow, the bubbles pricking her throat as they slid down, matching the prick at the backs of her eyes. 'I am.'

Tonight, as always, Paige felt absolutely ancient.

'Excuse me,' she murmured, rising and headed for the refuge of the bathroom.

Valentino watched his cousin dancing with his new wife, a gladness in his heart that Alessandro had finally found love after the train wreck of his first marriage.

It always humbled him when he saw two people ready to make a lifetime commitment. Sure, after an early escape he'd worked out it wasn't for him, but that didn't mean he didn't believe in it for others. His parents were, after all, still blissfully married after fifty years.

He spotted Paige making her way back to the table and he was struck anew by how not his type she was. The crimson dress outlined a figure that had more angles then curves. Her breasts were small, her body one long, lean line, and she moved with purpose rather than grace.

And yet…

He rose as she approached the table and held out his hand. 'I believe it's our turn.'

Paige's heart thundered. His gaze had tracked her from all the way across the room and her heart beat as if she'd just dashed one hundred metres in less than ten seconds. She looked up at him, caution wrangling with temptation. How easy would it just be to surrender? To forget her mangled heart and the type of man who had mangled it in the first place and succumb to the invitation in Valentino's eyes?

But Paige had never been into masochism.

She ignored his hand and headed towards the dance floor.

Valentino grinned. If she thought for a moment that he couldn't read every emotion, the battle in those large grey eyes, she was utterly deluded. He followed her to the floor, his gaze glued to the elegant length of her naked spine the dress afforded him, and wondered what it would take to convince her to let her guard down.

Paige reluctantly let him shepherd her into the circle of his arms. His big hand sat low, just above her butt and just this side of decent. It was firm and hot and she felt a lurch in areas that hadn't felt anything in a very long time.

Valentino felt resistance as he tried to pull her a little closer. 'Relax,' he murmured to her temple.

She jerked her head back slightly to forcibly remove the brush of his lips from her skin. Relax? He may as well have asked her to fly to the moon. She glared at him. 'Let's just get through this, okay?'

Valentino chuckled. Paige wasn't one for stroking egos. Another factor he was finding surprisingly appealing. He'd drifted through life never having to work for the attention of a woman—ever. From his mother to his sisters and cousins, to the girls at school and beyond, he'd always had them twisted around his finger.

He was starting to realise how boring, how predictable, his life had been.

They moved to the music and Paige automatically followed, her senses infused with Valentino's clean male scent. She sought desperately for something to say to instil distance, to break the hypnotic pull of the music and his warm breath.

Anything.

'So, Valentino, Alessandro tells me you are a co-chlear implant surgeon.'

Valentino smiled at her robotic question. He looked down into grey eyes that were averted to a point beyond his shoulder. That she could see over his shoulder was a first for him too. Most women he'd dated, apart from Adrianna, had been shorter. At six feet two, he still had a few inches on her but the fact that it would just take one tantalising tilt of her chin to claim her mouth was an intriguing proposition.

'Yes, Paige. Alessandro tells me you have a daughter who needs one?'

Paige stumbled at the mention of McKenzie, grateful for a moment that Valentino's body was there to lean into, to steady herself. But then aware, too aware, of the muscles beneath his shirt, the strength in his arms, the heat of him, the power of him.

'Yes,' she said, pushing away from his chest and holding herself as erect, as far away as was possible, which was severely hampered as the dance floor filled with other couples and they were jostled closer together.

'She's scheduled for two months' time.'

Curiously Paige found herself wanting to tell him about McKenzie, about her fragile health and the long road they'd both been on, but as much as she was desperate for conversation to maintain distance, the ups and downs of her life were not for public consumption.

'Is she a patient of Harry Abbott's?'

Paige's face lightened. Now, Harry, her boss, she could talk about. She could talk about him and his genius all night long. Finally she felt on solid ground. 'Oh, yes. Only the best for my little girl. Do you know him? He's an absolute pioneer in the field.'

Valentino smiled, amazed at the difference in Paige as passion filled her eyes and she came alive, her face animated. Is this what she would look like beneath him in bed? His hand tightened against her spine, inching her unresisting body closer.

'Of course.' He shrugged. 'Everyone knows Harry.' In fact, it had been Valentino's very great pleasure to finally meet the man a couple of months back during an interview.

Paige nodded. 'He's an absolutely magical surgeon, so clever and such a fair boss. And great with his patients. He insists everyone in the audiology department knows how to sign so the patients are at ease.'

She chatted away, finally comfortable in his arms. So comfortable, in fact, she didn't notice that the song ended and another began. Or that they were now so close their bodies rubbed deliciously against each other as they swayed to the tempo.

Valentino, on the other hand, had noticed. In fact, he could barely register anything else. Her chatter faded into the background along with the music as his body responded to the subtle friction of her dress against the fabric of his trousers and the waft of frangipani and woman lit a fire in his groin.

She shifted against him as someone from behind bumped into her and he almost groaned out loud. 'Paige.'

His voice, low and throaty, snapped her out of her prattle and she was instantly aware of the chemistry between them. The ache of her taut nipples as they chafed against the fabric of her dress and his shirt. The darts of heat radiating from the fingers of his hand on her spine, shooting waves of sensation over her bottom and the backs of her thighs. The heat in her pelvis stoked by the heat in his.

Her eyes locked with his, the lust, the intent in his espresso gaze frightening. She opened her mouth again to use conversation as a weapon to repel him, to push him away.

But Valentino got in before her. 'Do you think if you talk enough you'll be able to ignore what's going on here?'

Paige's eyes widened at his insight. 'I…I don't know what you're talking about,' she denied, feeling frantic, like a mouse on a treadmill set on maximum speed.

'Paige.' Valentino ground out her name as he flattened his palm against her spine, bringing them even more intimately into contact. 'I think you do.'

For a few seconds Paige wanted nothing more than to grind herself against him. It was an urge she had to suppress with an iron fist.

The music stopped and people clapped. She used the distraction to gather every ounce of willpower and step out of his arms. 'No. I don't.'

And she spun on her heel and got as far away from Valentino Lombardi as she could.

An hour later Paige couldn't take being sociable another second. She knew it was bad form to leave the wedding before the bride and groom but she just couldn't stand being in the same room as Valentino, watching him dance and flirt, for a second longer.

She made her apologies, assuring Nat she was staying the night but pleading a headache. When the lift arrived promptly she almost pressed a kiss to its cold metallic doors. The impulse was short lived as they opened to reveal Valentino, his jacket slung over his shoulder, his bow-tie undone, leaning against the back wall.

They stared at each other for what seemed an eternity. 'Going up?' he murmured.

Damn, damn, damn. Paige entered the lift after a brief hesitation during which an errant brain cell urged her to run. But she was damned if she was going to show this man he had any power over her. She turned her back on him, keeping to the front of the spacious lift, and searched the buttons for floor twelve.

Of course, it was already lit. Great! Same floor. Next they'd have adjoining rooms! The doors shut and she clutched her bag, reaching for patience.

Valentino, afforded an unfettered view of her spine, looked his fill. He couldn't deny he wanted to see more of her back. And her front. He wanted to see her become passionate and animated again. And not about a nearly seventy-year-old surgeon who was old enough to be her grandfather. But about him. And what he was doing to her.

But she'd made it perfectly clear that any attraction was not going to be acted on. Valentino Lombardi had never had to beg in his life—he wasn't about to start.

The lift arrived at their floor and Val smiled as Paige practically sprinted from it. He followed at a more sedate pace, not really wanting to know where her room was. What if they happened to be neighbours? Would knowing she was in the next room be any good for his equilibrium? Wondering if she slept naked? Wondering if she was as sexually frustrated as he that she might help herself to ease the ache?

He shook his head. *Dio!*

Except it seemed they were to be neighbours and if her cursing and muttering was anything to go by as she rammed the keycard in her door, he was going to have to lend a neighbourly hand.

He hung his jacket over his doorknob and strolled towards her, resigned to his fate. 'Can I help with that?'

Paige slotted the card in and out several more times, wanting to scream as she twisted uselessly at the handle. She turned to him, glaring like it was all his fault. 'I hate these things.'

Val smiled. She was animated when she was angry too. Her cheeks flushed pink, her chest rising and falling enticingly, grey eyes sparkling like headlights in fog. He reached for it. 'Allow me.'

Paige didn't protest. She couldn't as his scent infused her senses. She'd done it all back at the wedding. There was no more resistance left. His fingers were sure as they slowly inserted the card into the slot and slowly pulled it out again.

Would he be that slow with her? That thorough? The light turned green and she shut her eyes as he turned the doorknob and opened her door.

'*Entri.*'

Paige looked into her room. Her big empty room. She flicked her gaze to Valentino's big hands with his sure fingers.

Val was surprised by her hesitation and although he couldn't see her eyes he sensed the battle from earlier had returned with gusto. 'Maybe I could join you?'

Paige felt absurdly shaky inside. She wanted to cry, burst into tears. She hadn't realised how lonely the last couple of years had been until an attractive man had propositioned her.

She looked at him instead. Saw the naked desire heat his gaze. This was crazy. 'I don't…' What? Have sex? Make love to? What could she say without sounding gauche or desperate or like a sixteen-year-old who'd never been kissed? 'Sleep with men I've just met.'

After all, it had taken her three weeks and a handful of dates to succumb to her attraction to Arnie.

'I promise you, there will be no sleeping.'

Paige swallowed hard. Both at the gravel in his voice and the sincerity in his gaze. 'I don't understand,' she said. Her throat was parched as she fought a little longer, hoping the sexual malaise invading her bones would lift. 'Any woman in that room tonight would have accompanied you here in a flash—why the hell do you want me?'

Val gave her a lazy smile as anticipation built in his gut, his loins. 'Because you're the only woman who wouldn't have.'

So she was a challenge? She supposed she should have been insulted but funnily enough they were precisely the right words for him to use. It told her she was something to be conquered and discarded, like all the others. Which, contrarily, right now, suited her just fine. She didn't have time or room in her life for the distraction of a love affair. But she did have tonight.

Obviously the only thing he was interested in.

It was win-win.

Paige pushed off the wall and without saying a word brushed past him and entered her room. She hoped it looked confident and sexy and that he couldn't hear the boom of her heart or the knocking of her knees.

She stopped in front of her bed, opened her bag, took her mobile out, checked it for messages then placed it on the bedside table before tossing the bag aside. She heard the click of the door behind her in the muted light and didn't have to turn to know that he was walking towards her. And in seconds his heat was behind her, his breath at her neck.

He said nothing as his fingers stroked up her arms. Neither did she. Nor did she say anything when his hands peeled the dress off her shoulders, baring her to her waist.

But she did cry out when his thumbs swept across her bare nipples, already hard and eager for his touch.

And when he kissed her neck.

And when he whispered her name.

Paige woke disorientated to a warm hand laid possessively low on her abdomen and a strange buzzing as a pale dawn broke through the gaps in the heavy curtains. She glanced at the clock—five-thirty. They'd been asleep for thirty minutes—Valentino had been true to his word.

The buzzing came again and movement caught her eye as her mobile vibrated and moved slightly across the surface of the bedside table. It must be a text message.

It took another couple of seconds for the import to set in. A text message.

McKenzie.

Instantly frantic, she grabbed her phone and accessed the message, her hands shaking, her heart pounding.

McKenzie woken with a slight temp. Don't worry. Everything under control.

Paige read the message three times, feeling progressively more ill. Oh, God. Her daughter was sick again and where was she? In the arms of some Italian Lothario thinking only about herself.

She leapt out of bed, ignoring the pull of internal muscles, grabbing for her clothes, furious at herself and Valentino for last night. She should have followed her instincts and gone home. Not stayed. Not let herself be seduced into a one-night stand, no matter how amazing it had been. Seduced into forgetting about the one person who meant more to her than anything else on the entire planet.

Her baby was ill. She had to get to her.

She didn't even look at Valentino as she threw her things together in record time. Or as she fled the room.

As far as she was concerned, if she ever saw him again, it would be too soon.

CHAPTER TWO

PAIGE arrived for her last day of work before her holidays at St Auburn's, with a spring in her step. She hadn't had a spring in her step for a long time but it was there today. She couldn't believe that McKenzie's operation was just three days away now. Her daughter hadn't been unwell or had a fever since the night she'd slept with...since Nat and Alessandro's wedding two months ago, and she had even put on a little weight.

Things were finally looking up. Finally going their way. All she had to do was convince Harry to let her be in the theatre to observe McKenzie's operation on Monday and life would be complete.

A butterfly flapped its wings in her stomach as she rehearsed the words again. Not that Paige really thought it would be an issue. Yes, it wasn't usual but she knew Harry well enough to feel confident that he'd overlook the rules for his right-hand woman.

Paige was actually humming as she entered the operating theatre change rooms. Dr Gloria Reinhart, the anaesthetist Harry used for his lists, was changing into her scrubs and Paige bade her a hearty good morning.

'Morning,' Gloria said, staring at Paige, an odd look on her face.

Paige frowned. 'What?'

Gloria shrugged. 'Nothing. It's just that I've never heard you hum before.'

Paige didn't need a translation. She knew she was serious. That she wasn't much fun. She came to work, ran Harry's theatre and his clinics with ruthless efficiency, not particularly caring whether she made friends or not. She didn't socialise or have time for gossip or idle chit-chat.

She was respected. Whether she was liked or not hadn't been a priority.

Paige grinned. 'Well, it's about time that changed, don't you think?'

Gloria responded with a grin of her own. 'Past time, I'd say.'

They chatted while Paige changed into her scrubs and then went in different directions—Gloria to the staffroom for a cuppa with her colleagues, Paige to Theatre four to set up for the first case.

The theatre list was sticky-taped to the door of theatre four's anaesthetic room and Paige removed it. Not that she needed it, she knew exactly which patients were being operated on today. In fact, if pushed, she could probably recite the list for the next month, even though it was next Monday's she was the most fixated on.

There were two paediatric patients on the list this

morning. Children were always done first. It caused less stress for the parents, who didn't have to wait around all day worrying about their child going under general anaesthesia, and also for the children, who were often at an age where they were frightened of the clinical hospital environment and didn't understand why they couldn't eat and drink and run around.

A little thrill ran through Paige's stomach at the thought that, come Monday, McKenzie Donald would be first on this list and her spirits lifted even further. Paige couldn't remember a time when she had felt this positive. It had been a long hard three years with many a detour and roadblock. It was hard to believe the path was suddenly clear.

Theatre four was frigid when she entered via the swing doors and Paige rubbed at the goose-bumps on her arms. Soon she would be gowned up and under hot lights and wistfully remembering the cold, but for now it seeped quickly into bones that had very little covering insulating them.

You're too thin.

The words Valentino had uttered that fateful night as he had lazily run his finger up her spine crept up on her unexpectedly, as they so often did, echoing loudly in her head and sounding very close in the silence of the empty theatre. So close, in fact, she looked behind her to check he hadn't actually appeared.

Nope. Just her.

She shook her head and frowned. She'd thought about the man so much in the last two months it wouldn't have surprised her to have conjured him up. She'd tried, usually quite successfully, to pigeonhole her thoughts of him to night-time only, to her dreams, but sometimes they crept up on her unawares.

She should have been insulted by his assessment of her body but one look at the heat and desire in his eyes and she'd known that he hadn't been turned off. In fact, quite the opposite—he'd wanted her badly.

It was merely a statement of fact. She was thin.

She hadn't had much of an appetite since the twins had been born prematurely. Daisy's death, Arnie's desertion and McKenzie's fragile health had robbed what little had remained. She ate only to fuel her body, with no real enjoyment when she did.

All her energy was focused on getting McKenzie to eat. McKenzie's appetite. McKenzie's nutritional needs. McKenzie's caloric requirements. Paige Donald came low down on Paige Donald's list of priorities. And, besides, things just tasted so bland.

A hoot of laugher outside in the corridor pulled Paige out of her reverie and she pushed thoughts of Valentino aside. This was daytime. Tonight she could think about him again, dream about him again. Vivid dreams that woke her in a sweat with parts of her throbbing, his name on her lips, his taste in her mouth.

She busied herself getting the theatre set up, grabbing the trolleys and positioning them correctly around the operating table, wiping them down with a solution of surgical spirits. She exited the theatre via the back door into the sterilising room. Four sterilised trays wrapped in special blue disposable cloth were waiting for her and she grabbed the nearest, along with extra drapes and gowns and two pairs of size-eight gloves for Harry and his resident.

She dumped them on the trolleys inside the theatre, ready to be opened by the scout nurse while she herself was at the sinks scrubbing up. She went back out again, selecting other bits and pieces she knew Harry would need—suture material, dressings and, of course, the actual implant device itself.

Paige turned the boxed bionic ear around in her hands. It was hard to believe that something so innocuous could give such a precious gift. That come Monday one would be implanted into McKenzie's head. She hugged it to her chest, sending up a quick prayer into the universe.

Please let everything be okay.

She went back into the theatre, dropping the extras on the trolley. A noise from the anaesthetic room alerted her to Harry's arrival and she smiled. It was nice working for someone as dedicated as she was. Paige glanced at her watch. Now, while they were still alone, was as good a time as any to ask her boss the question.

She shoved open the swing doors with her shoulder, ready to launch into her spiel. Excited even. Except the man in the anaesthetic room wasn't Harry. He wasn't thin and a little stooped and grey-haired. He was big and broad with curls of dark hair escaping the confines of his theatre cap to brush the neckline of his scrubs. Even if she hadn't dreamt about that back every night for the last two months, the lurch low down in her pelvis would have alerted her to his identity anyway.

Valentino Lombardi looked up from the theatre list he'd been studying and turned. Neither of them said anything for a few moments as a host of memories bubbled between them.

Valentino swallowed. He'd been prepared to see her again but totally unprepared for the sucker punch to his gut as her big grey eyes, round with shock, met his.

'Paige. Bella. We meet again.'

Paige blinked. She even blushed a little as the things they'd done together made her awkward beneath his gaze. It didn't help that he filled out a pair of surgical scrubs better than any man on the planet.

She'd seen him in a tux and in the buff and now in a set of scrubs. Was there nothing the man didn't look magnificent in? 'Valentino?'

What did he think he was he doing here? Was he here to observe? To assist? Didn't he live in Rome? Or London? Where was Harry?

Valentino saw the confusion in her gaze and shot her a lazy grin. He'd relegated their one night two months ago to a pleasant interlude and done his hardest to forget about it. But standing before him now in baggy scrubs, no make-up, her hair covered in a sexless blue theatre hat, he finally admitted he hadn't forgotten one second of their time together.

A strange unease descended on them and he couldn't bear it.

Paige's heart skipped a couple of beats and then accelerated as his low flirty voice oozed into all the places that still craved his touch. The pinkness in her cheeks deepened as she remembered where his mouth had been. Oh, God! This wouldn't do at all.

'Dr Lombardi.' Paige's voice was stern as she glared at him and regained her composure. 'What are you doing here? Where's Harry?'

Valentino laughed. So much for small talk. He regarded her for a second. What he had to tell her next would have an impact on her probably more than anyone. Harry had stressed the need to break it to Paige gently.

'I'm afraid Dr Abbott had to rush to Hobart in the early hours of this morning. His grandson was kicked in the head by a horse and is in Intensive Care.'

Paige gasped, pressing a hand to her chest. Oh, no! How awful. 'Was it Andy or Ben?' Harry's daughter and her family lived on a horse stud just outside Hobart. They were a close-knit family despite the distance, and Paige knew this would be devastating for them all.

'Ben.'

Oh, dear, Ben was only four. One year older than McKenzie. Paige moved closer to him, needing to know more. 'How is he? Is he…has he…?'

Valentino covered the distance between them, reaching out for her, clasping her shoulders gently. 'He's critical. That's all I know.'

Paige looked at him, trying to process it. Trying to understand how fate could be so cruel to a little boy and a man who had only ever done good things. 'That's just so…awful. I can't believe it.' She shook her head to clear it, searching his espresso depths, waiting for him to tell her it was all a bad joke. 'I just can't…take it in.'

Valentino nodded. 'Yes.' What else could he say?

Paige wasn't sure how long she stood there, staring at him, trying to clear the block of confusion in her mind. But she suddenly became aware of the slow, lazy circling of his fingers against her upper arms and the clean, male smell of him. When the temptation to lay her cheek against the V of his scrub top came upon her she knew she had to step back.

Valentino released her and watched as she retreated to the nearby bench and leaned against it. 'I'll be covering Harry's patients until he's ready to return.'

It was then that the full impact of this incident hit home. McKenzie. She glanced at him sharply as her heart thudded like a rock band in her chest.

No. No, no, no.

Why? What had she done, what had McKenzie done to deserve such upheaval? The surgery had been delayed too many times already. So many things had gone wrong in her short life. The one constant had been Harry and his absolute faith that he could give McKenzie the gift of hearing that prematurity had robbed her of.

And now that was in jeopardy too. 'My daughter's surgery is on Monday.'

Valentino nodded. 'Yes. Harry mentioned that.' In fact, Harry Abbott had gone to great pains to explain to him that Paige would be understandably concerned and probably not all that happy.

Paige felt awful. She wanted to scream and rant and cry. For Harry as well as herself. Disgust built inside her too. How could she even be thinking of herself, of McKenzie, when little Ben was critically ill?

'It's okay. I'll do her surgery.'

Paige glanced at him sharply as a tense 'No' fell from her lips.

Val's jaw tightened. 'You don't think I'm a good surgeon?'

Paige had the urge to laugh hysterically. This was a truly bizarre conversation. She was having trouble keeping up. 'How do I know, Valentino? I don't know the first thing about you.'

Valentino raised an eyebrow. 'Really? I have one night that says differently.'

Paige slashed her hand through the air, rage bubbling inside that he would make an innuendo at such a time. 'You know I meant—professionally,' she snapped. 'Don't ever, ever, talk about that night again. Okay?' she demanded. 'Just don't.'

Valentino had every intention of talking about it again. In fact, standing before her, his loins stirring at the memory of them, he had every intention of doing it again. But he could see she was close to the edge and that night, for now, was better off left in the past. He put his hands up in front to calm her.

'I am a world-class cochlear surgeon. I'm head of the department in a large London hospital. I chair an international cochlear implant committee. I have performed this operation countless times on both children and adults. And…' he placed his hands on his hips '…I am a damn good surgeon.'

Paige shook her head, his arrogant stance and impressive credentials falling on deaf ears. He didn't get it. He just didn't get it. This was McKenzie.

McKenzie.

Her child. Did he think she would allow a total stranger to cut into her? Drill a hole in her head? Did he think that was an easy thing for her to consent to? Never mind allowing someone she didn't know to do it?

Still, she was torn. McKenzie needed the operation and if they delayed now, who knew how much longer it might be? Her heart broke, thinking about yet another delay for her beautiful baby girl locked into a world of silence. 'I'll wait. I'll cancel and wait for Harry to return.'

Valentino flinched inwardly, surprised that her rejection of his skills would feel so personal. He gave a stiff bow. 'Of course, that is your prerogative.'

Paige nodded. 'Yes.'

'It could be a long time,' Valentino murmured. 'Harry was talking about months, maybe a year if Ben needs extensive rehab.'

The thought of McKenzie waiting that much longer was like an ice pick to her heart. She wanted to weep and wail and beat her chest. She shrugged instead, struggling for nonchalance, the effort nearly killing her. They'd waited this long…

Valentino could see the abject disillusion written all over her face and shimmering in her big grey eyes. 'Why don't you hold off making a decision until after today? Watch me in action. Then tell me you don't want me to operate on your daughter.'

Paige couldn't believe he would think it was quite that simple. 'It's not just about that, Valentino,' she snapped. How were they supposed to have any kind of doctor/mother-of-patient relationship with their one-night-stand between them?

God, why had she been so impulsive two months ago? She was never impulsive!

Valentino regarded Paige, her implication clear. 'I will treat McKenzie like any other child who is a patient of mine.'

'And me?'

Valentino shrugged. 'Like any other mother.' Liar. He stood still, waiting for the thunderbolt.

'Oh? How many of the other mothers have you slept with?'

Valentino gave a grudging smile. 'I thought we weren't talking about that?'

Paige sighed, too weary and plain heartsick to respond properly. 'No. We're not.' She glanced at him, the epitome of cool, calm and collected, while she felt all at sea. There was still so much she couldn't wrap her head around. 'I don't understand how you're even here, now…in the country.'

'Harry interviewed me months ago. He's thinking of retiring—'

'Retiring!' Paige spluttered. 'He never mentioned retiring to me!'

'He's sixty-eight years old,' Valentino calmly pointed out.

'Yes, but…' Harry talked to her about everything. And he still had so much to give, to contribute.

'I've wanted to work in Australia for a while now,' Valentino continued, his gaze on the little frown nestled between her caramel brows. 'I think there are things I can learn here to take back home with me. I have my visa, all I need is the right job. I was attending a symposium in Melbourne—'

'"Bionic Ear in the Twenty-First Century?"' Paige enquired absently, not really caring. Harry had given a paper at it two days before.

Valentino nodded. 'Harry contacted me in the early hours of the morning and asked me to fill in. I got the five a.m. flight out of Melbourne.'

'Oh.' So they'd be working together too. This wasn't how it was supposed to pan out. None of it was. But, then, when had her life gone according to plan over the last three years? Bitterness rose like bile in her throat. Wasn't it her turn to catch a break?

Valentino pushed off the bench opposite, which he'd propped himself against, and took three paces until he was standing in front of her. 'Watch me today, Paige,' he murmured. 'Then we'll talk.'

Paige felt his husky tones wash over her, soothing the burn and the knot of worry that sat like an iron fist deep in her gut.

And before she could refute him, rebuff him again, he turned away and she watched as he exited the anaesthetic room.

So much for feeling positive. How could her day have gone to hell so early?

It took about ten minutes into the first surgery to convince Paige of Valentino's capabilities. He was, indeed, an extremely good surgeon. Efficient, steady, sure and capable. Methodical in his approach, supremely knowledgeable, unfailingly polite and, despite the mask and being covered head to toe in green, devilishly charismatic.

There wasn't one nurse he didn't flirt with, including Di Hamilton, who'd been married for thirty-five years and had twelve grandchildren. It was obvious he adored women and Paige watched as every female fell under his spell.

But he was a man's man too. From the nervous surgical resident who was assisting to the orderly adjusting the theatre light, he won them all over, talking football and Australian beers and the price of petrol.

They all loved him. Paige wished she could say the same. Between concentrating on her job, the thoughts circling in her head at a thousand miles an hour and the cataclysmic brush of his arm or fingers as she passed him an instrument, she was totally over him by the end of the day.

Every breath, every move, every chuckle or low request for something stroked along her pelvic floor and took her right back to that night. Being under him. The way he'd felt inside her. Which only agitated her even more. She had bigger things to worry about. Like poor Harry and his grandson. And McKenzie.

It was like she was in a bubble with him, just the two of them, everyone else fading into insignificance. She knew that was the way it often was between surgeon and scrub nurse, requiring a special kind of synchronicity. But it was more than that and she knew it. She'd anticipated Harry's every move in Theatre for the last two years but had never felt this more base reaction.

She just wanted out. To get as far away from St Auburn's and Valentino Lombardi as possible. To hug McKenzie and remember what was real in her life and what was fantasy.

When the last op was finished, Paige couldn't get out of her gown quickly enough. Thankfully Valentino had left the theatre to go and do post-op checks in the wards and she was able to breathe again. To function without a pulse that kept racing and a stomach that wasn't looping the loop. To clean up. To do her job.

She was back in the audiology department thirty minutes later, making notes in patient charts, very aware that she had the next six weeks off and conscientious enough to ensure everything was up to date on today's operative cases.

'Here you are. Gloria said you'd be here.'

Paige's heart gave a jolt and she braced herself as she looked up from her chart. He was lounging in the doorway in trousers and business shirt, open at the neck and turned up at the cuffs, looking dark and tousled and incredibly sexy.

'You have hat hair,' she commented, before casting her eyes downwards again.

Valentino chuckled, ruffling his locks. 'Yes.' He guessed that was one of the advantages to her pixie cut. Not a lot of hair there to get bent out of shape.

'I thought you might like to know that Ben's condition has stabilised a little.'

'Oh!' She glanced up quickly. 'What a relief!' She'd tried to ring Harry during the break between lists but had got his message bank. 'Thank you.'

If anyone knew what it was like to watch your child critically ill in an intensive care unit on life support, it was Paige. Her heart went out to Harry and his family. She didn't envy them the days ahead.

Valentino nodded. 'We're all going for a drink after work. Why don't you come? I can give you a lift if you like.'

Paige ignored the traitorous pull she felt at his invitation. Was he insane? 'Sorry. I can't.'

Valentino gave her a wry smile. 'Can't or won't?'

Paige shook her head. 'Can't.'

'Who takes care of McKenzie when you work?'

'My mother.'

'I bet she wouldn't mind staying on for an extra hour.'

Paige knew for a fact she wouldn't. But that wasn't the point. She wanted to see her daughter. She missed McKenzie desperately when she was at the hospital and resented the hell out of Arnie for putting her in a position where she had to work to support them both.

Paige took in the lazy grace with which he lounged in the doorway, the charming smile on his face and those dimples, which thankfully the mask had hidden all day. What did an Italian playboy know of her mundane, hand-to-mouth, practically housebound existence?

'Sorry. I can't.'

Valentino pushed out of the doorway and sauntered towards her. He placed two hands on the desk where Paige was sitting. From his height advantage he could see the ridges of her prominent collarbones. And the unlined curve of breast which told him she wasn't wearing a bra under her modest T-shirt. 'You know you want to.'

This close he looked better still. And smelled absolutely divine. She put her pen down and plastered a bored look on her face. 'I don't expect you to understand, with your carefree, different-girl-every-night lifestyle, but I'm a mother.' She said it slowly so he understood. 'At the end of the work day I go home to my child. I even look forward to it. That's what a parent does.'

Valentino gripped the desk hard. She was wrong. He did understand. There'd been a girl once, a long time ago. And, briefly, a baby.

He frowned. He hadn't thought about Daniella, about the baby that never was, in years. He pushed off the desk lest the urge to speak about it, to tell her he did know, overcame him.

He folded his arms. 'Suit yourself.'

Paige nodded. She intended to. His dimples and his

lazy lounging had gone and he was all dark brooding intensity. It was equal parts sinister and sexy. 'Hadn't you better be going?' she asked pointedly as the silence between them grew.

'I was wondering if you'd had a chance to think over McKenzie's operation?'

Had a chance? She'd thought about little else all day. And she knew she didn't have it in her to postpone again over something so petty in comparison to her daughter's deafness. Not when she had the services of a world-class surgeon and a place on his Monday-morning list.

Still, her pride, all she had left these days, made the words difficult and she hoped she wouldn't choke on them. 'Yes, I have.' She nodded, dropping her gaze to the top button of his shirt. 'I'll not be cancelling.'

Valentino regarded her for a moment. He could see how hard it had been for her to say the words. He hadn't wanted that. He'd sensed from the beginning that Paige was like a tightly coiled spring, just holding it all together. It wasn't his object to break her. Not like this anyway. 'Good. I guess I'll see you Monday morning.'

And he turned away, heading for the door.

'Wait.'

He turned back. She'd risen from her seat and was looking at him with desperation in her eyes.

'I need to ask you something. A…favour.'

Valentino clenched his fists at his sides. He could tell she was uncomfortable asking something that was obviously quite personal to someone who, apart from one frenzied night two months ago, was a relative stranger. 'Okay.'

'I want to be in there. With McKenzie.'

Valentino took a moment searching for a way to soften the instant denial that had sprung to his lips at her completely unethical suggestion. No wonder she'd looked so hesitant. 'Paige.'

'Not scrubbing in or anything. Just…there. Nearby.'

He searched her big grey eyes. Saw the worry. The anguish. '*Bella*, you know I can't allow that.'

Paige shut her eyes. This was so unfair. Harry would have. She felt like she was about to burst into tears and his endearment didn't help. She would not break down in front of him. 'Don't. Don't call me *bella*.'

'You need to be a mother on Monday,' he murmured. 'McKenzie needs you to be a mother.'

'Harry would have allowed it,' she said, defiance in her gaze.

'No, Paige, I doubt very much he would have.'

Paige swallowed hard. 'Please.'

Valentino wanted to go to her. He could see her struggle, knew this was difficult. But he could also see she wouldn't want his sympathy. He ground his feet into the carpet. 'Don't you trust me?'

Paige bit down hard on the lump in her throat. 'Of course I do.' And she did. She knew McKenzie was safe in Valentino's skilled hands. But she'd never been apart from her, had been by her daughter's side through all her ups and downs. She couldn't let her go through this momentous surgery all alone.

'Then let me do my job. And when it's over, you can do yours.'

Paige swallowed another block of emotion welling in her throat, desperate to persuade Valentino. 'Is this about the drinks?'

Valentino stilled, her implication smarting. His eyes narrowed as he tempered his words. 'Be very careful, *bella*. I don't like your insinuation.'

To her horror a tear squeezed out before she could blink it away and she was as vulnerable and as exposed to a man as she'd ever been. Not since Arnie had walked out on her after Daisy's death had she felt so completely at the mercy of a man.

What did he want? Did he want her to beg?

That she wouldn't do.

Valentino stepped towards her as the tear trekked unhindered down her cheek. 'Paige.'

She dashed it away and held out her hands to ward him off. 'Go. Just go, damn it!'

Her words pulled him up short and as much as the doctor in him urged him closer, the man knew she was only just holding it together and the last thing she'd want was to break down in front of him.

He nodded. 'See you Monday.'

Paige waited for him to leave before flopping back in the chair and bursting into tears.

CHAPTER THREE

PAIGE was finger painting with McKenzie when the doorbell chimed on Sunday afternoon.

Who on earth could that be?

She just didn't get visitors, other than her parents and they'd left a few hours ago. And if she did, she liked to have prior knowledge, screen them first. The days of people just popping in were long gone. Even Nat knew to call first before she brought Juliano around for a play.

Paige tried to control, as much as she could without making her daughter a virtual prisoner, the numbers of people she exposed McKenzie to. The more outside contacts, the greater the risk to McKenzie's less than robust immune system. Paige knew only too well that a mild illness a normal toddler could shake off in a few days usually landed McKenzie in hospital on a drip.

She knew people thought she was a control freak but she could live with that.

'Coming,' she called as she quickly washed her hands under the tap in the kitchen. It was probably somebody trying to sell her something and with the operation tomorrow weighing heavily on her mind she really didn't have the patience for it.

She yanked open the door, mentally drawing herself up to give the person on the other side the thanks-but-no-thanks-now-go-away spiel and shut the door on them as quickly as possible.

Except Valentino Lombardi smiled down at her, dimples a-dazzling, and Paige felt her chest deflate. He was wearing faded blue jeans, a white T-shirt and wicked aftershave. His hair was damp, curls clinging to the back of his neck, as if he'd not long been out of the shower.

It made her excruciatingly aware of her own rumpled state. Baggy trackpants and a tatty oversized T-shirt falling off her shoulders and streaked with paint. 'Oh.'

Valentino quirked an eyebrow. She had a smudge of dried red paint on her cheek. He liked it. 'You were expecting somebody else, yes?'

Yes. Anybody but you. She frowned. 'How do you know where I live?' Had he been following her?

Valentino grinned. 'Alessandro.'

Of course…Paige made a mental note to call Nat and ask her not to give out her address to Italian Lotharios.

Valentino noticed the tightening of her lips. 'Don't be cross with them. I told them I wanted to meet McKenzie before the surgery tomorrow.'

McKenzie chose that moment to appear, grabbing hold of Paige's leg with her paint-smeared fingers and shyly looking up, all the way up, at Valentino. Paige shifted slightly to accommodate her daughter, her hand automatically going to cup the back of McKenzie's head.

'Ah.' Valentino smiled. He crouched down so he was

at eye level with the diminutive little girl. As her chart had indicated, she was thin but her eyes were bright and intelligent. 'Here she is.' He signed as he spoke. 'Hello.'

McKenzie's eyes, so like her mother's but framed by blonde ringlets, widened for a moment before she shyly signed her greeting back.

'I'm Valentino.'

Watching McKenzie's tiny fingers form all the letters that made up her name always clawed at Paige's heart and today was no different. Had she known her daughter would be deaf, she would have chosen a much shorter name.

'Hello, McKenzie,' Valentino signed back, speaking the words also. 'I'm very pleased to meet you. You have paint on your nose.'

Paige watched as McKenzie, shy by nature, actually grinned at Valentino as he gently swiped at it with his finger. She could see the same sort of recognition in her daughter's gaze that she'd seen in other females whenever he was near. An awareness of him as a man, a purely feminine response to his charisma.

For goodness' sake, she was three years old! Did the man have to charm every female he came into contact with?

Paige drew her daughter closer, her hand firm on McKenzie's shoulder. 'Do you usually make house calls?'

Valentino grinned one last time at McKenzie and rose to his full height. Paige was annoyed. But, then, when wasn't she?

'No.'

'Then why are you here? You could meet my daughter tomorrow morning on the ward.'

Because Harry had asked him to speak with her. And he had agreed, even though he knew Paige was big trouble. Her appeal to him the last time they had been together, her pride, as tears had shone in her eyes, had captivated him. He should run a mile. He didn't do this. He didn't get involved. Yet he'd thought of little else except her all weekend. And then there was Harry.

But not yet.

'I wanted to see you were okay. After Friday.' He held up a bottle of wine and a brown paper bag. 'I brought a peace offering.'

Paige stiffened. Did he really think she could relax over a glass of wine with him? 'There was no need. I'm fine.'

Fine she may be but all Valentino could see was a woman who was starving, both physically and emotionally. Shutting herself off, denying her body the things it needed. The things every body needed. Denial was not good for anyone.

He crouched down to McKenzie again. 'What do you say, McKenzie?' he said as he signed. 'Can I come in?'

McKenzie smiled at him and nodded, holding out her multicoloured hand. He took the little girl's offering and rose, quirking an eyebrow at Paige.

Paige glared at him. 'That was low.'

He smiled and took a step forward as Paige fell back passively, like she feared his nearness. He took full advantage as McKenzie led him into the apartment. 'You need to eat,' he said, moving past her. 'Lucky for you I've found the most amazing delicatessen near where I'm staying.' He looked down at McKenzie and moved his hands as he said, 'Kitchen?'

Paige stared at him as McKenzie pointed and then happily led Valentino to where he wanted to go. How had that happened? It was a few moments before she registered the drift of Valentino's chatter coming from the other room and the fact she was still standing like a powered-down robot in the hallway, staring after them.

She sighed and shook her head as she followed. How long would it take to get him out? By the time she'd reached the kitchen Valentino had seated McKenzie on the bench beside him, poured two glasses of wine and was supervising as her daughter distributed a variety of olives into little bowls.

She leaned against the jamb. 'Making yourself at home, I see.'

Valentino looked up at an unsmiling Paige. Her shirt had fallen off a shoulder and he could see the distinctive hollow above the bony ridge of her collarbone. He also noticed the lack of bra strap. Not that he could make out anything interesting beneath the shapeless shirt.

'McKenzie is very helpful.'

It was strangely sexy to see him in her kitchen, laughing with her daughter. His broad shoulders stretched the confines of his white T-shirt as his hip rested casually against her counter. Even more sexy was the way he signed and talked without conscious thought, as if it was completely natural.

McKenzie, noticing Valentino's interest had wandered elsewhere, turned and grinned at her mother, and Paige's heart rose in her throat. Her daughter never took to anyone this quickly. Trust her to take to a guy who, like her father, was never going to stick around.

Absently she noticed that Valentino had had the good sense to wash the paint off McKenzie's hands first.

Valentino removed the still warm baguette from the bakery bag. 'Ah.' He held it to his nose and inhaled the yeasty fragrance. *'Quello sente l'odore di buon.'*

He offered it to McKenzie to smell as well, which she did mimicking him perfectly. 'You like?' he signed, and McKenzie nodded. He located a knife in a drawer near his hip and sliced the bread into thick discs before arranging them on the plate next to the olives.

'Is there somewhere we can eat this?'

Hell!

Paige, also used to signing and speaking while her daughter was around, followed his lead. 'Will the deck be good enough for your lordship?'

He looked at McKenzie and winked. 'Perfect.'

Valentino scooped McKenzie off the bench and she skipped after her mother the second her feet touched the floor. He loaded the food and wine onto a nearby tray and followed the women through the house.

They passed through an airy lounge room cluttered with children's toys and framed photographs. Valentino's gaze fell on a largish one standing on top of the television. It was Paige with an older couple. Her parents? She was younger, her figure fuller, rounder, no angles. Her hair in a caramel bob. And she was laughing, her grey eyes lit with an easy humour.

Interesting.

His gaze returned to her as she stepped out onto the deck, her back ramrod straight, very different from the relaxed woman in the picture. Although it was lost in the fold of a voluminous shirt, he still remembered how her back had looked, long and elegant, bare to the hollow, on the night of Alessandro's wedding.

Still remembered running his fingers down the naked length of it as they had danced, and the way her breath had caught, the ragged edge to her breathing.

Heat in his loins had Valentino gripping the tray a little harder and searching for something to take his mind off how well he knew every inch of her body.

Not just her back.

'Does she know about tomorrow?' he asked as Paige indicated for him to take the seat opposite her at a sturdy wooden table.

Paige glared at him as she made room for McKenzie on her chair. 'Of course.'

Valentino ignored the steel in her voice and the seating suggestion as he sat himself at the head of the table closest to her. If he had to force-feed her, she was going to have to be within arm's reach.

'Okay,' he said, plonking the tray between them and handing her a glass. 'Do you want to tell her who I am?'

Paige took the glass automatically. It was a perfectly sensible idea. She'd put off telling McKenzie that Dr Harry wouldn't be doing her surgery until bedtime. Now, particularly as McKenzie seemed quite ena-moured with Valentino, seemed as good a time as any.

'McKenzie?' Paige touched her daughter's arm.

'This is Dr Lombardi.' She spelt out each letter of his name even though she knew that at three McKenzie had no concept of spelling.

McKenzie looked at him. 'Valentino,' he reiterated, signing his first name.

Paige bristled. 'Dr Valentino,' she corrected, her voice firm, her signing slashing at the air. 'Dr Harry had to go and visit his grandson who is very sick so he can't do the operation to make you hear again. Dr Valentino is going to do it instead.'

McKenzie looked from her mother to Valentino and back to her mother. 'Dr Valentino is going to make me hear?' she signed.

Valentino looked at Paige, saw the way she nodded confidently, even though her eyes were worried.

'Yes,' she said.

McKenzie turned to look at him with her big blue eyes as serious as her mother's. After a moment she transferred her gaze back to Paige. 'Okay,' she signed, and reached for a piece of bread.

Paige blinked. That had been easy. McKenzie adored Harry. Trusted him. He'd been her specialist for over three years now, since her diagnosis in the NICU, and she loved it when he came to visit her in hospital. Paige glanced at Valentino, searching for a reason. He looked up at her simultaneously with dark espresso eyes and smiled at her, dimples on high beam.

Her stomach looped the loop. Could it be that simple?

McKenzie tugged her arm and she dragged her gaze from his. 'Can I watch *The Wiggles*?' she signed.

She nodded and said, 'Sure.'

McKenzie climbed off the chair and Paige followed her inside to set up the DVD, thanking modern technology and *The Wiggles* for their special DVDs for deaf kids, complete with Auslan interpreter at the bottom of the screen. Just because her daughter was profoundly deaf, it didn't mean she didn't like to wiggle with the rest of the toddlers.

Paige smiled as McKenzie's curls bounced and she laughed at something the red Wiggle had said. But beneath her smile was profound sadness that McKenzie couldn't even hear the sound of her own laughter. Only the prospect of tomorrow, of starting a whole new chapter, dragged Paige out of her gloom.

Valentino watched an even more subdued Paige walk back towards him. She pulled up her chair, picked up her glass and absently swallowed a mouthful of the crisp Pinot Grigio he'd chosen because it came from the area near where he'd been born in the north of Italy. There was no recognition on her face of the glorious crisp, spritzy taste.

He picked up the plate of olives and brought them close to his face, inhaling deeply. 'Hmm. Don't these smell divine?'

Paige looked at the plate with disinterest. 'I'm not hungry,' she murmured.

Valentino smiled. It was going to be fun reviving her appetite. 'Who says you have to be hungry to eat?' He picked up an olive glistening with oil and stuffed with feta and sucked it into his mouth. 'Food is to be enjoyed, *bella*. Not endured.'

Paige watched as the olive disappeared from sight behind Valentino's plush lips, leaving the merest trace of oil smeared on his lips. It was a compelling sight.

'Try one,' he coaxed.

Paige, forgetting that her daughter was nearby, suddenly knew how Adam had felt when presented with the apple. She'd bet he hadn't been hungry either. 'If I do, will you just go?'

Valentino grinned. 'Soon.' He presented the plate to her and nodded encouragingly.

Paige rolled her eyes. Anything that got him and his dimples out of her house soon was worth a try. She selected the same kind he had from the array of plump specimens on the plate. She popped it into her mouth, chewed it twice and swallowed it. 'Happy?'

Valentino tsked. 'You need to savour it, *bella*. Inhale its aroma.' He picked one up and waved it under his nose, inhaling deeply. 'Roll it around your mouth.' He sucked it in with a satisfying *phft*. 'Let it sit on your tongue,' he murmured, shutting his eyes as the salty flavour fizzled on his taste buds.

His eyes fluttered open to discover her gaze firmly fixed on his mouth. Her black pupils had dilated in the grey pools of her eyes and his breath became constricted in his lungs.

He pushed the plate closer. 'Try again.'

Paige shook her head as his low murmur wrapped seductive tentacles around her pelvis. As if seducing an olive with his mouth hadn't been bad enough. 'Are you always this bossy?' she grouched.

Valentino stared into her eyes. 'You are beautiful but you need to eat more.'

Paige let her gaze drop to the array of olives, embarrassed by his empty compliment. She hadn't felt beautiful in for ever. 'I'm just not hungry any more. Not since...'

Valentino heard the catch in her voice. Understood her silence. It may have been a tiny blip a long time ago which he'd buried beneath wine, women and song, but he understood loss a little. 'Since your daughter died.'

Paige nodded slowly as her gaze drifted back to his face. 'Alessandro?'

Valentino inclined his head. 'He mentioned it.'

He seemed so empathetic, his dark eyes soft like velvet. But how could he possibly know? 'I wouldn't expect you to understand.'

'I understand some.'

He held her gaze for a moment or two and then dropped it to the plate and picked up an olive. 'Be careful of this one, it still has its pit.' He presented it to her mouth and pushed it gently against her lips, stroking it against them. 'Don't be deceived by its plainness. The buttery flavour is truly sensational. Creamy. Seductive.'

No one was more surprised than he when she sucked it into her mouth with no protest. She started to munch and he put his finger against her lips. 'No. Don't. Stop. It's not popcorn. Let it sit in your mouth. Savour it. Roll it around. Tell me what you taste.'

Paige was as surprised by the request as she was by the fact that there was even an olive in her mouth in the first place or that his finger rested tantalising against her lips. She pulled back slightly. 'It's just food.' She shrugged. 'It tastes like food.'

Valentino sighed and shook his head. 'Shut your eyes.'

'What?' Did he think she was mad? 'No.'

Valentino almost shook her from pure frustration. 'Just shut your eyes,' he implored, bringing a hand up to gently shutter her lids.

Paige wanted to tell him to leave. To pull away. But his fingers were incredibly slick from the olive oil and wonderfully fragrant.

'Now, tell me what you taste.'

Paige knew he wasn't going to let this go so she took a moment to tune into the olive sitting in her cheek. She pushed it onto her tongue as he had suggested and mentally homed in on the taste. 'Salty. But smooth, like thick double cream.' She opened her eyes, surprised at herself.

Valentino smiled. 'That's the spirit.' Not giving her a chance to change her mind, he reached for another. A black Kalamata marinated in herbs. 'What about this one?'

Paige closed her eyes again to block out the image of him as he inched it towards her. Her nostrils flared as it slowly moved towards her. What was that herb? Rosemary? Her stomach rumbled.

Valentino pushed the olive past lips that parted slightly at the merest touch, like a flower to the first rays of the sun. A little burst of heat fizzed to life in his loins. The oil moistened her lips and the urge to follow the path of the olive with his own mouth was an urgent thrumming in his blood.

Paige bit into the flesh, bruising it a little, and let out an almost suppressed 'Oh' as a burst of flavour exploded against her palate. Rosemary and chives and something else. Something spicier. Her lids snapped open and Valentino was so close, so sure. Maybe the spice hadn't been in the olive at all.

'Hmm.' She licked her lips and got another burst of flavour. 'That is good.'

Valentino sucked in a breath. She had no idea. Oil still smeared her mouth and he wanted nothing more than to relieve her of it. Their gazes locked as memories of their night together were suddenly thick between them.

'That's nothing,' he said, dragging his eyes away from her face that was a delightful mix of uncertainty, confusion and newly discovered pleasure. 'You have to taste this camembert. It's incredible. So rich and creamy.'

He loaded up a piece of bread with the soft cheese. 'Did you know,' he said as he presented it to her, 'that you shouldn't have cheese on crackers? It should always be eaten with bread?'

Paige eyed the loaded offering coming closer and knew from the still frantic beat of her pulse she couldn't let him feed her again. She reached out and took it from him, suddenly too hungry to deny herself but not stupid enough to invite liberties that she wasn't free to give.

Valentino watched as she took a bite. 'Remember, slowly. Let it melt against your tongue.'

He watched and waited. Waited for the cheese to hit her taste buds and for her to realise she'd been starving for too many years. When her eyelids briefly closed, he knew he had her.

'Good, isn't it?' He smiled as he reached for one himself. 'The aroma is intoxicating, yes?'

Paige had to agree. Intoxicating. Yes. Just like him. But, seduced as she was, she knew she was treading on very dangerous ground with him. Too dangerous. She savoured the bread and cheese and washed it down with a mouthful of wine that suddenly seemed to sing in her mouth.

Valentino smiled at her and she knew she had to put a stop to it. 'What are you really doing here?'

Still he shied from the information he'd come here to impart. 'I told you. I came to meet McKenzie.'

Paige raised an eyebrow. 'Really?'

Valentino made them another cheese offering each and pushed hers towards her. 'And to, how do you say, clear the air? Set the ground rules. We're going to be working together in the coming months, whether you like it or not.'

Paige stilled. Ben? She sat up straighter. 'You've heard about Ben, haven't you?' Harry had spoken with her briefly on Friday night but she hadn't been able to get hold of him since.

Valentino nodded. 'He has a significant brain injury. They don't think it's fatal but there will be considerable…deficits. They are expecting a lengthy rehabilitation period.'

Paige searched his face for the truth of it. The

horrible, horrible truth of it. That's why he'd come. 'You could have rung.'

Valentino shook his head. 'I think you are very close to Harry. I knew you were worried. I didn't want to tell you over the phone.'

Paige nodded absently, knowing it was kind, appreciating it on some level. Poor, poor Harry and little Ben. A deep well of sadness opened inside her and she was quiet for a moment, her thoughts troubled.

After a while she looked at Valentino and it suddenly sank in. For the short term, he was her new boss. They were going to be working together. And he wanted ground rules.

Well, good, she had a couple of her own.

She narrowed her eyes. 'Number one ground rule. We're never going to be…' She broke off, shying from the intimacy of the word.

'What, Paige? We're never going to be what?'

Paige glared at him. He knew exactly what. Did he think she was some shy, wilting Victorian virgin? That she couldn't say the words? Her chin rose defiantly. 'Lovers. Again.'

Valentino smiled. He had to give her points for guts. 'Agreed.' He tended to keep his relationships short and sweet and this one reeked of complicated so her rule suited him.

He made another cheese and bread combo and handed it to her, gratified to see her eat it without protest. 'So let's just be friends. I'm going to be your boss. Your daughter will be a patient of mine. It wouldn't be right to be anything other than colleagues. Friends.'

Paige stared at him. He could seriously do that? 'We can do that? You and I?'

'*Naturalmente.*'

She shot him an incredulous look. 'Do you have many female friends?'

Valentino chuckled. Already she knew him surprisingly well. 'Women love me,' he evaded with a knowing grin.

Of that she had no doubt. Paige laughed in spite of it all. In spite of having an impossibly sexy man right in front of her who she knew carnally and who had just admitted his track record with women didn't usually run to friendship.

She should have been running a mile.

But being friends would certainly make the time until Harry came back to take over McKenzie's care easier. And it would make working for him a lot smoother. She and Harry worked well together not just because she respected his abilities but because she liked him.

Except, of course, Harry had ever seen her naked…

But surely she could have the same kind of relationship with Valentino? If they worked at it. They were both professionals after all.

Paige offered her hand. 'Okay. Friends.'

Valentino looked at her hand. 'In my country we're not big on handshaking,' he teased. 'We prefer to kiss.'

Paige rolled her eyes but kept her arm fully extended. 'There's a shock. Just as well we're in my country, then.'

Valentino chuckled and enfolded her hand in his. 'Friends.'

Paige nodded as a flush of heat spread up her arm and coursed through her system. Not a very good start…

The next morning McKenzie was happily ensconced in a bed in her own private room at St Auburn's. She was comfortable here, her home away from home, unworried as she watched television that she couldn't hear but engrossed nonetheless. Paige sat by her side, her heart splitting in two, her heart palpitating wildly every time she thought about her daughter's imminent surgery.

She'd wanted this. She'd wanted it for so long. But now it was here, it seemed too much. Too much for a little girl who'd already been through enough. She was jumpy and nauseous. Her empty stomach growled at her and she ignored it. She just hadn't been able to face the usual piece of toast she forced down every morning.

'Buongiorno.'

Paige turned to find Valentino lounging in the doorway. He wore dark trousers and a deep green business shirt with a paisley tie. He looked relaxed and confident and was like a sudden balm to her stretched taut nerves. She shot him a strained smile.

'McKenzie?' Paige touched her daughter's arm.

McKenzie looked away from the television and her face broke into a wide smile as she waggled her fingers at an approaching Valentino.

Valentino grinned back. 'Are you ready?' He signed as he spoke.

McKenzie nodded and when he held out his hand to her, she high-fived him. Valentino dropped his gaze to Paige, who was currently shredding a tissue into a million pieces. He placed his hand gently on her shoulder and gave it a squeeze. 'How are you?'

Paige bit down on her lip hard. She would not cry. She just wouldn't. She looked up at him. 'Terrified.'

He could see that. He gave her a gentle smile. 'I'm going to take very good care of her.'

Paige nodded. Too emotional to speak. Too scared to open her mouth lest she break down.

'Here,' he said, thrusting another one of those brown paper bags at her. 'I brought you some *biscotti* from the deli. It's to die for.'

Paige frowned and took it automatically. 'I really couldn't eat a thing.'

'You have to pass the time somehow. You may as well eat really good food.' He winked at her, keeping it casual, upbeat, even though he wanted to gather her close and whisper assurances in her ear until she relaxed. But he sensed she was barely keeping herself together and he didn't want her falling apart before it had even begun.

'See you after the op,' he murmured, before swaggering out of the room.

Three hours. Three interminable hours later they pushed a sleeping McKenzie, her head swathed in bandages, back into her empty room, accompanied by a nurse. Paige, who had gnawed through half of the *biscotti* out of sheer nervousness, felt all the worry fall away like the *biscotti* crumbs as she stood. Relief coursed through her, strong and sweet. Her legs wobbled and she grabbed hold of the bedrail.

Paige's breath caught in her throat as she surveyed her daughter. For a moment, lying so still and pale against the white hospital sheets, McKenzie looked like her sister. Memories of Daisy swamped her, those last horrible days rising large in her mind as an awful feeling of dread rose in her chest.

Was McKenzie even breathing?

The nurse busied herself around the bed as Paige leaned over her and pressed kisses to her daughter's face so different without her blonde curly halo. She needed to touch her, needed to know, to be sure.

'McKenzie,' she crooned.

McKenzie stirred, her eyelids fluttering open for a second. 'Hello, baby,' Paige whispered.

She dropped her forehead onto her daughter's chest, shutting her eyes, riding the surge of release as the cold, hard grip of worry slackened its hold. McKenzie's heartbeat coursed strong and sure against her forehead and it was instantly comforting.

It was well after lunch before Valentino joined them. Paige knew there was only a morning list today and had expected to see him some time in the afternoon.

'Hi,' he whispered, approaching quietly.

Paige looked up. He was wearing the same clothes as earlier *sans* tie, showing off the golden skin of his neck. She had the strangest urge to press her face to it.

'Hi,' she whispered back, not wanting to disturb a sleeping McKenzie.

Valentino crouched down beside her. 'It all went really well. In a few weeks we should be able to switch the device on.'

Paige nodded. His voice was a low murmur and she was suddenly overwhelmed by the gift his skilled fingers had given his daughter. She'd been sitting here for hours, trying not to think about it, trying to concentrate on the here and now. But Valentino had opened the door.

A rush of emotion swamped her chest and she could feel her eyes filling with tears. 'Thank you,' she whispered.

'Hey,' Valentino crooned as tears spilled down her cheeks. Her face crumpled and he pulled her head onto his shoulder. 'It's okay.'

Paige nodded as a sob escaped. Then another. For the first time in years she actually felt as if it was really, actually okay.

And she had him to thank for it.

CHAPTER FOUR

TODAY was the big day.

It was totally surreal for Paige. She walked into St Auburn's, McKenzie in tow, pressed the lift button for the fourth floor, stepped out, turned right and walked through the open doors marked Audiology.

It wasn't any different from what she'd done three days a week for the past couple of years.

Except it was. Everything was different.

Today was the day they'd know whether the operation had been a success or not. Today was the day McKenzie would hear.

A week ago Valentino had seen McKenzie for her routine two week post-op check. He'd been pleased with her progress and they'd set this date for the activation of the device.

'Hi, Paige. Hello, McKenzie.' Greg Palmer, the team's social worker, was first to greet them. He grinned at McKenzie as he signed. 'Today's the day, huh?' he said to Paige.

Paige gave him a tight smile as McKenzie went

straight to the corner of the large entrance lounge to where she knew the puzzles were kept. 'Yes.'

He squeezed her arm. 'It'll be fine.'

Paige nodded as she pressed a trembling palm against her stomach. Of course it would be okay. 'I'm a little early. Is Ellen in yet?'

Greg frowned. 'I think Valentino's going to do the honours.'

'Oh.' She hadn't counted on that. Ellen was one of the two audiologists in the department and today was her day on, so Paige had just assumed...Valentino must have made room in his schedule to be there for McKenzie.

The knot of nerves in her belly twisted even tighter.

Today, if all went according to plan, was probably going to be quite emotional. And she'd cried in front of Valentino once too many times as it was.

'I think he's already in his office.'

Paige shot a nervous look towards Harry's office. *Valentino's office.* She wanted to go in, was eager and excited on one hand but scared and nervous too. What if they got no result?

'Go,' Greg urged, squeezing her arm again. 'It'll be fine.'

Paige took a deep breath and nodded. 'Come on, McKenzie,' she said, crossing the room to her daughter and crouching down next to her. 'Let's go and see Dr Valentino,' she said as she signed.

McKenzie smiled at her and took her hand and they headed for the door behind which lay a whole new life. Paige knocked lightly and entered at Valentino's command.

Valentino looked up from a pile of charts on his desk as Paige's deer-in-headlights eyes sought his. He knew all about the squall of emotions going on inside her. Had seen it on hundreds of parents' faces as the big moment arrived.

She looked tired, dark shadows beneath her incredibly huge eyes making them appear even more stark in her face. Her clothes, as usual, were two sizes too big, skimming the bony angles of her body, hanging instead of hugging. Had she eaten any of the goodies he'd had delivered to her house every day for the last few weeks?

'Paige,' he said, standing, denying the dictates of his body urging him to go to her. He transferred his attention to McKenzie instead. 'Hello, there.' He grinned. 'Are you ready?' She nodded and he signed, 'Come in.'

Paige held fast to her daughter's hand and didn't move. 'You don't have to do this. Ellen will be in soon. You have surgery.'

She didn't know why she was so resistant to Valentino switching on the implant. A few weeks ago she wouldn't have cared less had it been a trained monkey. But this man, this sexy Italian playboy surgeon, was different. There was more than a professional connection between them, no matter how they tried to avoid it.

There was intimacy. And Paige knew from bitter experience that intimacy left you vulnerable. Something she swore she'd never be again when it came to men.

She doubted it would have mattered had she not slept with him. But she had. And while he was obviously a pro at separating himself from that, standing before him now, she knew she couldn't.

Valentino shrugged. 'I had a cancellation.'

Paige frowned as she searched her memory for this week's theatre cases. 'Who?'

'Paige.' The reproach in his voice was heavy. 'You're off duty, remember?'

'I know. It's just…' Paige didn't understand why she just couldn't let it go. Why she was resisting. 'That's why we have two audiologists so the surgeon is free to operate.'

'And miss the pay-off? This is the best part of my job, Paige. That moment when my patient hears something for the first time. It's what makes it all worthwhile.'

Paige felt humbled by his response. And petty for equivocating. Every day since McKenzie's surgery tempting edible treats had arrived on her doorstep. From flaky pastries to scrumptious pizzas to the richest of chocolates. All from Valentino.

She'd been trying to dismiss him as a charming, love-them-and-leave-them pretty boy but how could she when confronted not only with his gifts but his heart-felt words? He was a great surgeon, good with his patients, excellent with their mothers and obviously emotionally invested in the gift he gave.

After everything he'd done for her, could she really deny him the rewards?

McKenzie spied the low kiddy table strewn with puzzles and tugged on Paige's hand, dragging her into the office. Paige let an eager McKenzie go and shut the door behind her.

'Why don't you sit down with McKenzie while I get set up?'

Paige nodded and walked on wobbly legs to the table, sitting on the child-size chair beside her daughter.

'Has she had any repetition of those earlier dizzy episodes?' Valentino asked as he tapped away at his computer.

'No.' The first few days post-op Paige had noticed McKenzie would stagger a little on standing. She hadn't been concerned, knowing it was directly attributable to the disruption of the inner ear and they'd settled quickly.

Valentino pressed one last key on the laptop and glanced at Paige. 'Okay. Ready. Let me check how the wound's doing first.'

He got up from his desk and took the seat on the other side of McKenzie. He tapped her hand and when she turned to him he signed and said, 'How is your ear, McKenzie? Can I have a look, please?'

McKenzie nodded her agreement and cocked her head to allow him access. He lifted the angelic curls that covered her right ear out of the way to expose the small shaved area where he'd operated. Two weeks ago there'd been some slight swelling over the bony area behind her ear but now it looked normal. 'It's healed beautifully,' he murmured.

He let her hair flop back over the site. 'Okay, then,' he said to Paige, but signed for McKenzie's benefit. 'Let's fit the external component.'

Paige nodded, apprehension swirling in her gut. 'Dr Valentino is going to fit your new hearing aid,' Paige signed.

Not that it was the type of hearing aid that McKenzie

was used to but having worn them most of her life it was the simplest way to explain it to a three-year-old.

McKenzie kept playing as Valentino fiddled with the external component, fixing it directly over the area where he'd implanted the internal part. It was a small circular unit that consisted of a microphone, a speech processor and a transmitter. It linked magnetically to the internal mechanism, which consisted of a receiver and a stimulator.

He then retrieved his laptop from his desk, and set it up at a smaller desk directly behind where McKenzie was sitting. He fiddled some more, plugging the external component into the laptop via a long cord.

'Okay, you know the drill now,' Valentino said. 'I'm going to run the neural response telemetry first. It should take about ten minutes. She won't be able to hear this.'

Paige nodded. She knew that Valentino would pick a few of the electrodes now implanted into McKenzie's cochlear to stimulate via the computer. He would get a reading back which told him that the auditory nerves had responded.

Unlike hearing aids that magnified sound, the cochlear implant directly stimulated the auditory nerves inside the inner ear.

The minutes seemed like hours as the silence in the room built. The urge to drum her fingers on the table was like an itch and she deliberately tucked her hands in her lap.

Valentino nodded. '*Buon*. Good,' he murmured.

'The nerve is responding perfectly so we know the implant's working.'

A rush of adrenaline kicked in at Valentino's confirmation and Paige gripped the table as she gave him a tight smile. She'd been having nightmares that they'd get to this point only to find the implant was a dud.

The first hurdle had been surpassed!

Valentino saw the slight sag to her shoulders and a flicker of relief light her profile, and despite the battle raging inside over professional distance he reached out and gave her shoulder a quick squeeze before returning his hand to the keyboard.

'Okay, I'll switch it on now. Yes?'

Paige nodded. This was it. This was the moment. One or two clicks of the mouse and her daughter should be able to hear sound.

Paige looked so tense Valentino wondered how much longer she could go before she snapped in two. 'It's important not to expect miracles,' he murmured gently. 'A lot of children don't react—'

'I know that,' Paige interrupted. *Just do it!*

'I know.' He nodded. 'But I'm going to go through it anyway. It's different when it's your own child.' He waited for her to protest and when she didn't he continued. 'McKenzie may not do anything at all once it's switched on. That's common. It's hard to know with little ones what they're hearing, particularly if they're pre-verbal or have been deaf all their lives as McKenzie has. They don't even know what sound is.'

He stopped and checked that Paige was with him

and then continued. 'I have it on very low so sudden noise doesn't frighten her, but she could cry. That's quite a common reaction.'

Paige nodded again, pleased suddenly that Valentino had taken the time to mentally prepare her for the range of possibilities, even though she knew them back to front. The fantasy in her head was very different from what would probably happen so it was a good reminder.

'Yep. Okay.'

'This is just the first step. It's going to need several mapping sessions as well as intensive speech therapy to train McKenzie's brain to recognise the sounds she'll hear as speech and to learn to talk herself.'

Paige nodded again. 'I know.' She was prepared for the long haul.

'Why don't you sit opposite her and then we'll start.'

Paige rose and moved to the other side of the table. McKenzie, engrossed in her puzzle, didn't even notice.

Valentino clicked the mouse a couple of times. 'It's on. Why don't you try calling her?'

For a few seconds Paige wasn't capable of speech. Of anything. She'd been looking forward to this moment for the last two years and now it was here she was totally overwhelmed. Just like that. One click and a whole new world for McKenzie. It seemed like such an anticlimax. Surely it should at least be heralded by trumpets. Or angels?

A swell of emotion rose in her throat and stuck there, her heart beat like an epileptic metronome, her lungs couldn't drag air in and out fast enough.

'It's okay, Paige,' Val murmured as he watched her emotional struggle. 'Take your time.'

Paige glanced at him. He was smiling at her encouragingly and she swallowed hard. He was obviously well used to the raw emotion of the moment.

'M-McKenzie.' Her voice shook and she cleared her throat. 'McKenzie, darling, can you hear me?'

McKenzie played on, blissfully ignorant to sound or to her mother's turmoil. Paige flicked her gaze to Valentino.

'It's okay,' he said. 'Keep on going. I'll keep adjusting it louder.'

A part of Paige was desperate to gesture to McKenzie, gain her attention. This was the biggest test of both of their lives and Paige couldn't believe how much she wanted her daughter to pass. But pre-empting the process by letting McKenzie know she was speaking to her was pointless—they were after an uncoached reaction.

'McKenzie? I love that puzzle you're doing, sweetie. It's just like that one we have at home with the koalas, isn't it?'

The silence in the room reached a screeching crescendo. She raised her eyes to Valentino, her heart beating so loudly now in the utter silence she thought it might explode out of her chest. 'Nothing.'

The air of helplessness in the word was heartbreaking and surprisingly Val felt Paige's anguish deep in his gut. When had this little girl and her mother become so personal?

He shot her his most comforting smile. 'The telemetry is telling me her nerves are being stimulated. You

know sometimes it can take a few weeks for kids to recognise any useful sound.'

Paige nodded, her lips pressed tightly together. She
did know. But still she felt gutted.

'I'm going to try clapping.'

'Okay.' Paige tried to keep the dejection out of her
voice and failed.

Valentino gave three loud claps. Paige watched as her
daughter startled and swiftly turned her head in the direction of the offending noise. She gasped as tears
rushed to her eyes.

She'd heard! McKenzie had really heard.

After three years of living in a world where no noise
existed, McKenzie could actually hear.

If someone had asked Paige to describe the emotion
threatening to suffocate every cell in her body she
wouldn't have been able to. She was totally overwhelmed. It was a miracle.

A miracle!

Valentino grinned at McKenzie. 'Hello. Did you hear
that?' he signed, and clapped again. 'Clapping,' he said,
and did it once more.

McKenzie swivelled her head to look at her mother.
The expression on her face was one of pure wonderment. She pointed to Valentino and clapped.

Paige laughed through her tears, dashing them away
with the backs of her hands. Her daughter looked like
she'd just invented clapping. Like she was the only
person on earth who could hear! And Paige knew
exactly how she felt.

'Well, I think that was fairly definite, yes?' Valentino smiled.

Paige nodded wildly, even though her face was threatening to crumple. Her deaf daughter could hear. It was simply the most amazing thing she'd ever witnessed. Even though she'd been present through so many activations in her two years with Harry, this time it was simply incredible.

She rose from her chair and in three paces was by McKenzie's side, picking her up, kissing her face, rocking from side to side. She wanted to spin and twirl, dance like a mad thing, but was aware of the cord attaching McKenzie to the laptop.

Still McKenzie rocked enthusiastically and giggled, holding tight to her mother's neck, enjoying the ride. Paige laughed too, giddy with joy and hope, lighter than air.

'It's amazing. Amazing, amazing, amazing!'

Valentino chuckled. 'Yes, it is.'

Paige slowed and pulled McKenzie against her for a long hard hug. Valentino was watching them with a big smile, dimples on high beam. Even sitting in his chair, he looked big and broad. His long bronzed fingers rested against the keyboard.

Fingers that had given the gift of hearing to her daughter.

'Thank you Valentino. Thank you,' she said over McKenzie's head. 'I don't know how I could possibly thank you enough. Words just seem…inadequate.'

Valentino dismissed her words with a quick wave of his hand. McKenzie's reaction, Paige's reaction, had been thanks enough. He grinned at her. 'I have a great job, don't I?'

Paige grinned back. 'Yes, you do.'

McKenzie squirmed and Paige realised she was still holding her tight. 'Sorry, darling,' she said, lowering her to the floor. McKenzie went back to her puzzle as if nothing momentous had happened and Paige laughed again.

Valentino adored the sound. It was quite melodious and he realised he hadn't heard her laugh, truly laugh with joy and abandon, until now. He guessed she hadn't had a whole lot to be happy about in the last three years. He was glad to have been instrumental in it.

'I like hearing you laugh,' he murmured.

Paige dragged her gaze away from her daughter, sobering a little. He was staring at her mouth and there was intenseness in his espresso depths. Her stomach muscles undulated as if he'd brushed seductive fingers against her belly. 'It's nice to have something to laugh about for once.'

Valentino nodded. 'Shall we continue?'

Paige drew in a suddenly husky breath. 'Please.'

That evening Paige flopped down on her couch utterly exhausted. Who'd have thought excitement could wear you out? They'd spent the rest of the day at her parents' place, watching McKenzie like a hawk, engaging her as much as possible, trying to gauge the extent of her new-found ability.

On the whole there were no major changes to

indicate anything had changed. McKenzie didn't seem to respond to their voices but Paige had no doubt now that would come. Towards the end of their visit, however, McKenzie did, very obviously, hear the crash when her grandfather accidentally dropped a metal bowl on the kitchen floor, turning instantly towards the sound and running to the kitchen to check it out.

They spent a hilarious hour dropping as many non-breakables on the floor as possible and revelling in McKenzie's amazed reactions. It was like watching her discover the world for the first time and Paige seriously doubted she'd ever tire of it.

There was a long way to go. She knew that. But today had been a resounding success and as she propped her feet up on the lounge, McKenzie tucked up safely in bed, Paige could honestly say she was content.

She sighed and shut her eyes, weary beyond belief but with a smile on her face. This had been an absolutely fantastic day!

The sharp peal of the doorbell startled her. Who on earth could that be at…she checked her watch…eight o'clock? She groaned. It was only eight o'clock? It felt like three in the morning.

Paige struggled out of the chair, a feeling deep down in her gut intensifying the closer she got to the door. It couldn't be? Could it?

She eyed her standard trackpants and baggy top and briefly wished she was wearing something different. More…feminine. But a spurt of irritation overrode it. She wasn't dressing to please him. And if he was going to keep turning up on her doorstep unannounced then he could take her as he found her. At least she had showered. She yanked open the door.

Valentino smiled down at her. 'Minestrone!' he announced with a flourish.

Her irritation dissipated instantly. She couldn't be cranky with him. Not after today. And he was wearing blue jeans and a snug-fitting T-shirt, his damp hair curling on his nape. 'Are you trying to make me fat?' she grouched.

He lifted the lid off the bowl and brought it close to her face. Mouth-watering aromas wafted her way. 'Yes, *tesoro*. That's exactly what I'm trying to do.'

Paige's stomach grumbled as the smell enveloped her in a warm cocoon. Every day for the last three weeks some sumptuous dish or other had been delivered to her doorstep. It seemed tonight was to be no different.

Except for the personal delivery.

'Let me guess. Mrs Agostino at the deli?'

Valentino gasped and clutched at his chest, feigning injured pride. 'Made it myself. One of my mamma's recipes.'

A man who could cook? Arnie had been the laziest man on the planet. Charming but utterly useless. She hadn't noticed it in the beginning but then their lives had taken a dive and Arnie had not risen to the occasion.

Just when she thought he was like her ex, Valentino went and did something that surprised her. Paige opened the door wider. 'Come in, then.'

She led him to the kitchen, reaching up for two

bowls. She heard the scrape of glass against marble and turned to see him pouring two glasses of red wine the colour of ripe mulberries.

He held it out to her and she almost refused. McKenzie would no doubt wake at some stage during the night, as was her usual pattern, and be up early, as bright as a button. And she was really out of practice with drinking wine. But today he'd performed a miracle and she would have drunk out of a poisoned chalice right now if he'd offered it to her. So she took it.

Valentino smiled and lifted his glass. 'To McKenzie.'

Paige shook her head. 'To you.' And she clinked her glass against his.

They ate their bowls of soup sitting on the lounge. She only half filled hers, giving Valentino the lion's share. But when she'd finished she'd wished she'd kept a little more for herself.

Valentino had been tempting her palate so much these last few weeks she was actually noticing flavours and textures again. Her appetite was hardly normal but instead of ignoring her stomach when it grumbled she actually went looking for something to put in it. Lucky for her, with Valentino's edible gifts hanging around, there was plenty of choice.

She looked longingly at Valentino's bowl. He lifted his eyes from his food and looked at her and she quickly dropped her gaze. But then she noticed how his jeans moulded to powerful quads and she remembered how they'd felt beneath her fingers and she quickly looked away. Thank God she'd had the sense to sit on the cushion furthest away from him on the three-seater after he'd chosen the single lounge chair.

'Would you like some, *bella*?'

Startled, Paige glanced at him. The look on his face was one of pure innocence, the soup bowl thrust towards her. But his eyes and the slight lift of his mouth told her he was perfectly aware of the double meaning.

'No. I'm really full.' Her stomach growled at her loudly as if in protest and she blushed as he chuckled, placing her hand on it to calm the recalcitrant beast.

She was never hungry. Or at least hunger was so inconsequential in her life; she never paid it any heed.

She grabbed her barely touched wine and took a sip. 'So, this is your mother's recipe? What's that herb I can taste? It's so fragrant but I'm afraid I'm out of touch with all things culinary.'

'Basil.' Valentino watched her as she took another sip of wine, her lips pressed against the glass. 'Fresh basil, straight from the pot. My mother always says when in doubt add basil.'

Paige smiled. When he was sitting here like this in her lounge room she could almost forget he was a smooth, seriously sexy playboy with a girl in every port. That he'd dated a supermodel. It was like he was just an ordinary Joe, enjoying a quiet evening at home.

Oh, dear. She did not like the direction of her thoughts. Next she'd be convincing herself she could change him.

Because that had worked so well with Arnie.

'Your mother's deaf, right?'

Valentino nodded. 'Since birth. Maternal rubella.'

Paige nodded slowly. 'So you've always signed?'

'*Si.* I've been signing since before I could talk. We all can.'

'All?'

'Me, my father, my five older sisters. Even Alessandro.'

Five sisters? No wonder he knew women. She'd bet her last cent he'd charmed every one of them. 'Was that hard? Growing up with a deaf mother?'

He shrugged. 'It was the way it was. I never really thought about it. I'm sure it was a lot harder for her, having six kids to manage.'

'So you speak two languages and sign in them as well?'

'I sign in three actually. I had to learn BSL, British sign language, when I went to London and then when I came here I had to learn Auslan, although it is very closely related to BSL so that was reasonably easy.'

Damn it, did the man have to be so perfect? She folded her arms more tightly across her stomach. 'Has your mother ever expressed a desire to have an implant? She must be a perfect candidate.'

Valentino nodded absently. Paige had pulled the fabric of her shirt taut across her chest and suddenly he could see a lot more. Like she wasn't wearing a bra. Suddenly their decision to be friends was making less sense.

'She is. And I really want her to have one but she doesn't. She doesn't see that there's anything wrong with her. She has a full life, she can communicate and is quite active in the deaf community back home.' He shrugged. 'And I respect that.'

'Does that make me an awful person, then? Do you think by going down this path with McKenzie, my daughter will think that I think something is wrong with her?' She searched his face for an answer. 'Is it wrong of me to want this for her?'

Valentino frowned. He sat forward and placed his bowl on the table. 'Of course not, Paige. My mother is a firm believer in doing what you feel is best. As am I. Implants just increase options for the deaf. She would be proud of you.'

Paige felt a trill of pleasure squirm through her belly at the thought of Senora Lombardi's approval. 'I bet she's proud of you.'

Valentino grinned. 'But of course. Tells everyone about her son the surgeon.'

Paige laughed. 'That sounds familiar in any culture.'

Valentino regarded her for a few moments. 'There it is again,' he murmured. 'That laugh.'

She grinned. 'It might actually become a habit.'

Valentino's gaze flicked to her shirt where it had fallen off one shoulder and her nipples made two points against the fabric.

Friends, friends, friends.

He returned his eyes to hers. 'Wouldn't that be nice?'

Paige sobered. Very novel. He held her gaze and it was like being sucked into warm dark mud. 'Did I thank you enough? Really, Valentino, I don't know how to thank you enough.'

He shrugged. 'It's my job. I'm just lucky to have the best job in the whole world.'

'Still…' On impulse she stood and took a step towards him. And then another, until she was standing in front of him. 'Thank you so much,' she whispered. Leaning down, she slid her hands to cup either side of his face, her fingers pushing into the luxury of his hair, and pressed her mouth to his in a brief kiss.

It wasn't meant to be sexual. It really wasn't. It was meant to be grateful and heartfelt. A thank-you kiss from the bottom of her soul.

Friendly.

Quick in and quick out.

But she should have known she was playing with fire. Because her senses were filled with him. His food offerings had awakened them to flavour and aroma and texture and she was experiencing them all—his warmth, the scratch of his stubble and the clean male smell of him—and even though she pulled out of the kiss she was incapable of moving away.

Valentino looked up at her. Her eyes had gone smoky and just before she'd covered his mouth, her baggy shirt had fallen forward and he'd feasted his gaze on her pert naked breasts.

It hadn't been something a friend would do.

He was already hard for her as he reached out and encircled her wrists with his fingers.

Paige looked down at where his thumbs ran a lazy path over her pulse points. There was a brief moment when it was possible to back off, to remember that they'd decided not to do this again. But it passed. And then she was sinking her knees into the leather either side of his thighs, straddling him, settling herself against him.

And then they were kissing. Like the world was about to end. And then her shirt was off and his mouth was on her breasts, sucking her nipples deep into his hot mouth, rasping his tongue around them as they peaked and surged against its boldness.

And then his shirt followed and she was reaching between his legs, unzipping him, touching the hard edge of him, rubbing herself against him as she freed him from the prison of his underpants.

'Oh, God,' he groaned, thrusting himself into her hand. 'Condom?'

Paige slowed.

What?

Condoms? Of course.

Her heart was racing as she tried to order her thoughts. But then Valentino sucked a nipple into his mouth and she clung to his shoulder as her brain turned to mush.

'Condom,' he said again, releasing her thoroughly worshipped nipple.

Paige sucked in a breath, pushing her hands into his hair. 'I don't have any.'

Valentino groaned into her neck. At home he had boxes of the things. Not that he'd used one of them since coming to Brisbane. They pulled apart and looked at each other, heaving in oxygen, their chests rising and falling, sexual frustration adding to their agitation.

They looked at each other for about ten seconds and

then they were kissing again, touching, rubbing, sighing, moaning.

And somehow, Paige wasn't quite sure how afterwards, he manoeuvred her trackpants off and then he was in her, thrusting up as she ground down, and they were panting and calling each other's name and it felt good and right and the consequences be damned.

CHAPTER FIVE

VALENTINO had no idea how long it took for them to bump back down to earth. It was a slow realisation. A creeping awareness of the jut of her hips in his palms, the weight of her head against his shoulder, the slight brush of her lips against his collarbone as her breathing returned to normal.

He shifted slightly and murmured, 'I guess there is one advantage to having a deaf child.' He felt Paige smile against his skin and chuckled.

Paige, malaise heavy in her bones, couldn't move. It was warm and cushioned against his shoulder and she felt as if she'd been stroked all over with a thousand velvet fingers. The fact that they were still joined and he was still hard inside her was another incentive not to move.

Although if she did this…

'Don't do that,' Valentino groaned, clamping his fingers on her hips harder, holding them still. How could he possibly still be so hard?

'What? This?' Paige undulated her hips again and felt the full length of him glide erotically against sensitised tissues.

Valentino felt his breath strangulate in his throat. 'Yes. That.'

Paige smiled again, suddenly getting a second wind. She pushed away from his shoulder, her nakedness on full display. She looked down at herself, at how wanton she was, how not herself.

She'd always hated her breasts. They'd always been small and with her weight loss even more so. But tonight they looked one hundred per cent female, the pale blush of her nipples darkening and puckering like raspberries beneath Valentino's rapt gaze.

She arched her back a little and Valentino pulsed inside her. He didn't seem to find them wanting.

Further down she could see his fingers spread wide against the angles of her hipbones, bronzed against her paler skin. She could feel them holding her firmly, holding her close, branding her. His thumbs circled lazily, stroking the sensitive skin where her hip sloped to her belly.

Lower still she could see where they were joined. Where they became one. The most intimate of connections. It was hot and slick, tingling with the remnants of their joining and the hard hot length of him still buried inside her, and Paige undulated her hips again.

This time Valentino thrust a little and she gasped. 'Hmm, that feels good,' she murmured.

Valentino shut his eyes and nodded, slowly pulling out a little and pulsing back in one more time. 'How about that?'

Paige bit her lip as the fuse sparked to life. 'Really good.'

He opened his eyes and watched as her high breasts bounced a little. 'And this?' He leaned forward and took a nipple in his mouth, his tongue mimicking the torture of the deep slow thrusting down lower.

Paige whimpered and stabbed her fingers into his hair, grasping a fistful and pinning him there. Her hips moved of their own volition and he thrust up again as she slid down.

Valentino moaned, releasing her breast, his eyes shutting as his forehead dropped to her chest. Their bodies seemed to find a rhythm together and he was powerless to resist the pull of it. They were barely moving at all but she was tight around him, holding him inside, massaging his length with subtle flexions and slow pulsations creating a wonderfully erotic friction that stoked a furnace deep in his belly.

He slid one hand to her naked bottom, pressing her closer, and the other up her back until his hand cupped her nape, his fingers furrowing into her hair. His lips brushed her chest, her collarbone, the hollow at the base of her neck.

She whimpered at the back of her throat and he could feel her trembling. Could feel a corresponding quivering of his own muscles as a climax that had been on a slow burn ignited to full throttle.

When she gasped and threw her head back his hand slid to her shoulder and he pulled her closer still, their joined bodies slick with heat and sweat as they rocked.

'Valentino,' Paige cried, as her orgasm broke and she bucked against him.

'Yes,' he groaned. *'Quello è ritiene così buon.'*

Paige had no idea what he'd just said and neither did she care. It was low and husky in her ear and then she was sucked back into the vacuum where only they existed and pleasure was the only purpose.

Valentino looked up from fixing his clothes. Paige was dressed again and watching him with strands of passion still decorating her gaze like dewy cobwebs. She smiled at him and he realised he could get used to that look.

Kiss it goodnight every evening.

Wake up to it every morning.

His smile faded a little as a frisson of unease crawled up his neck.

Because there was no denying in such a short time he had felt a connection with Paige. Even just today, they'd been through so much. Witnessing McKenzie's reaction to his clap had been incredibly satisfying. And talking about his mother this evening had been…nice. Normal. What couples who dated did.

What couples did, full stop.

Not what he did. He didn't do couple stuff.

Not since…

And then there was what had just happened between them on the lounge. Twice.

What the hell was he thinking?

Paige picked up their bowls off the coffee table, the movement of her thoroughly ravaged body shrouded beneath her baggy sexless clothes.

It was a timely reminder that she wasn't the usual

type of woman he did this with. Despite the sexual gratification shimmering in her gaze. She was a single mother with a high-needs child. She had commitment written all over her. She was a couples woman. Or at least she deserved to be.

And this was the second time they'd got naked together. It was starting to feel like something a little more serious than what he usually went in for.

He didn't have a script for that.

Not any more.

'We can't do this again,' he said.

Except all he could think about was doing it again. Stripping those godawful clothes away and doing it in every room in the house.

And then maybe come back and do it all again tomorrow. *No. No. No.*

Paige blinked, setting the dishes down. Okay.

She knew he was right, of course but, deep in her heart a little dent appeared. She shrugged with as much nonchalance as she could muster. 'Of course.'

Valentino blinked. Well, that was easy…

In his experience women didn't usually take those five words all that well. 'I don't really do anything serious,' he explained, not really understanding why he felt the need to clarify things. 'And I think it's a bad idea for colleagues to get too involved.'

Paige suppressed a laugh. He hadn't been too worried about it thirty minutes ago. But he was certainly running now! Looked like the playboy had reached his end game.

Well, that was okay. Or it would be. This had only

ever really been one thing. A thank-you kiss that had got way out of control.

Just as well, though, she hadn't expected anything from him. That Arnie had hardened her heart to romantic nonsense and that she didn't have the time or the energy for someone else in her life. How many women had he devastated with that turn of phrase? She could well imagine how some dates would not take it so well.

'I agree.'

Valentino nodded, his hands on his hips, waiting for the *Oh* that usually came in this part of a conversation he was especially good at.

It didn't come.

He decided to explain further. 'I think we're adult enough to accept this for what it was.'

Paige suppressed a smile. 'It's okay, Valentino. I understand. Neither of us do this.' She gestured back and forth between them. 'I can't and you choose not to. It's fine.'

He opened his mouth to protest her assessment but he couldn't. He did choose not to. Since Daniella.

This was what he did. This was what he was used to.

'So…colleagues? Friends?'

She quirked an eyebrow. 'We're back to that again, huh?'

'You think you can't do it?'

'Oh, I can do it.' Did he seriously think she had time to sit around pining after him? She stuck her hand out. 'Can you?'

Valentino regarded her outstretched fingers. Remembered how they'd felt digging into his back. 'But of course.' And he clasped her hand in his and gave it a firm shake. 'I'll see you at the clinic tomorrow.'

Paige followed his broad back to her front door. He seemed to take up all her hallway and as some internal muscles protested her movement she was reminded of how big he was everywhere.

Valentino pulled the door open, paused and turned. 'What if there are consequences?'

Paige regarded his serious face with a sinking feeling. Somehow, even without the dimples, it looked as sexy as hell. She didn't like the direction of his thoughts.

Paige sighed. 'It'll be fine.' She hadn't had a proper period since the twins had been born. She doubted she'd even ovulated regularly the last two years due to her borderline weight.

She probably had the fertility of a panda.

'It's…safe?'

She knew what he was asking and it was an assurance she felt one hundred per cent comfortable with giving, even though they both knew, as medical professionals, no time was one hundred per cent safe. 'Yes. It's safe.' Still, she found it difficult to meet his gaze and she looked out at a point beyond his head, to the darkness of the street.

Valentino reached forward and lightly grabbed her chin, directing her gaze back to his. He fixed her with a stare. One that told her he meant business. 'I want to know, Paige. If…'

The mere thought of it was so painful Paige couldn't even contemplate it. She certainly was clueless to the slight edge of menace in his tone, to the fierce light in his eyes. Even mentioning it without actually saying the word was enough to fracture the surface of her heart and she shut her mind to it, blocked it like a force field.

'It'll be fine,' she repeated, before stepping back, causing his arm to fall by his side.

There would be no pregnancy.

Valentino regarded her for a moment or two longer before delivering a slight bow and disappearing into the night.

The next few weeks flew by. Life was fuller, crazier than normal. Further mapping sessions of McKenzie's implant and twice-weekly speech therapy chewed up her remaining three weeks at home.

But the rewards were amazing. After a few days it was evident that McKenzie heard just about everything and it was like witnessing the world being created all over again, seeing her wonderment of it all.

Instruments in the toy box that had merely moved in the past now made noise. The drumstick did more than bounce off the taut surface of the bongos—it actually bonged. The tambourine did more than shimmy—it rattled. And the sleigh bells tinkled.

But not just that. The doorbell chimed. And the plughole sucked and gurgled greedily as the water swirled away. And the television talked to her. The Wiggles talked to her! Every sound was new and amazing.

In the beginning she'd caught McKenzie just looking at objects that created noise, as if expecting them to get up and produce sound completely unaided. But she'd caught on quickly and no object was safe.

Her speech had also come on. In just a few weeks she already had a handful of words. Paige had never dared hope for the day that she would hear her daughter say 'Mummy'. But she had. And it had simply been the best moment of her life.

McKenzie still signed as she spoke—they both did—and Paige wondered how long it would be before her verbal communication skills were such that they outstripped her signing vocabulary. They would always need to sign as McKenzie was still deaf without her external device so it was vital to keep up their signing vocabulary as well.

And, anyway, being bilingual was such a skill—Valentino being a classic example—it would be a shame to lose it.

Before Paige knew it, it was time to go back to work, which she did reluctantly. Every minute with her daughter as she discovered a whole new world was precious and Paige resented having to surrender any of them.

Sure, McKenzie was in good hands with her parents but that didn't stop the gut-wrenching emotion she felt as she kissed her daughter goodbye three mornings a week. The only consolation was she still got to see McKenzie when she came in for her speech therapy and she made sure she scheduled her daughter's appointments for the days and times she was on the clinic.

There had to be some advantages when you ran the show.

Three weeks in and everything was back running like

clockwork. The op had been successful, intensive therapy had been instituted and the care arrangements clicked smoothly back into place. And McKenzie hadn't been sick in months. There was even some roundness to her face for a change, although Paige didn't hold too high a hope for cracking the twentieth percentile any time soon.

She and Valentino had even managed to find a happy medium in their relationship. She'd expected it to be awkward at first, like the day they'd first met again after that fateful night, but they'd both been invested in making it work. And he was great with McKenzie, who had also learnt to say 'Dr Valentino' very quickly.

Finally there'd even been encouraging news with little Ben, who'd been transferred out of Intensive Care and admitted to a specialist acquired brain injury rehab ward.

Things were great for once. All the planets were aligned. The gods were smiling. Life was good.

And then it all went to hell.

The last day of her third week back started as an ordinary day. Nothing remarkable. Until she was standing in neck-to-toe green, masked and hatted, waiting for Valentino to finish drying his hands and gown up, and a strong urge to go to the toilet gripped her bladder.

She frowned as she mentally suppressed the urge. For goodness' sake, she'd already been three times this morning already. Once when she woke up, once when she got to work and just prior to scrubbing up. How on earth could she possibly want to go again?

And, anyway, she couldn't just walk out of the theatre

and go to the bathroom. She was scrubbed, sterile. It would require degowning and then rescrubbing and re-gowning, and with theatre times tight they didn't have the luxury of running on the whims of her bladder.

She gritted her teeth and ignored it, holding the cuff of Valentino's glove open ready for him to thrust his hand straight in.

'Thanks,' he murmured as he repeated the process on the other side.

Paige could tell by the smile in his eyes that his dimples would be flashing beneath the mask. Normally that would be exceedingly distracting, despite their de-termination to keep things asexual, but today, as her bladder twinged again, it didn't even rate.

She clamped down on the sensation, trying for mind over matter as the three-hour operation stretched in front of her. There was no physical way her bladder could be full again.

She'd had a glass of water with breakfast and that had been it. Years of working as a scrub nurse had taught her not to drink tea or coffee prior to commencing surgery for just this reason.

It wasn't physically possible to have anything in her bladder. Surely?

Maybe she had a urinary tract infection? But no. It hadn't stung or burned at all. Fever? She did feel hot but she was swaddled in a gown, under bright operating lights and holding her muscles so tight she was probably overheating every cell in her body.

Or maybe it was some kind of delayed cystitis from

that night a few weeks ago? Valentino's arm brushed hers and for a sweet second she was back on his lap again.

Ten minutes later, though, she knew she couldn't hold on any more. She was actually crossing her legs beneath her gown. 'Darren can you scrub in, please?' she asked, hoping the discomfort in her abdomen wasn't detectable in her voice. Darren was one of the two scout nurses on for the theatre today.

Valentino, who was just preparing the drill, stopped and looked down at her. 'Everything okay?'

She nodded as she passed him the next instrument. 'Fine.'

The five minutes it took for Darren to wash his hands, re-enter the theatre, dry his hands and gown up felt like an hour as her bladder stretched to painful proportions. 'Excuse me for a moment,' she murmured stepping back from the table and degloving and degowning as quickly as possible without looking like her underwear was on fire.

She made it to the bathroom in record time and had never been more pleased to sit on a toilet in her whole life. So when the sum total of fifteen mils was forthcoming Paige was totally unimpressed.

What the hell?

After a further ten minutes of sitting was no more productive, Paige finally gave up. She washed her hands in the sink, inspecting her face in the mirror. The hollows beneath her cheekbones seemed more pronounced in the harsh fluorescent light. Maybe she did have a UTI? One that just involved frequency? Or maybe a kidney stone was blocking the neck of her bladder, only allowing a dribble through at a time? A painless one?

Hell, maybe she was the only woman on the planet to be in possession of a prostate gland?

She shook her head and watched her reflection follow suit. Maybe it'd be okay. Maybe it wouldn't happen again. Maybe she was going crazy and she should get back to work and stop worrying about something that was probably nothing.

She hurried back to the theatre, washing her hands again before donning a mask and pushing through the swing doors. Valentino and Darren both looked up as she entered.

'You want to scrub back in?' Darren asked.

Paige shook her head. She didn't want to risk it. 'You keep going. I'll scout.'

Which ended up being a wise decision. Paige spent the entire day in and out of the toilet. She may as well have stayed at home for all the help she'd been. And when the last patient was wheeled out of the theatre to Recovery she'd never been more pleased to clock off in her life.

She changed into her civvies, grabbed her handbag out of her locker and hurried back to Audiology to update the day's operating charts. The department had shut for the day and was deserted, for which she was grateful as she steamed into her office and made a quick phone call to her G.P.

This situation was ridiculous and needed remedying as soon as possible. She was put on hold straight away and Paige tapped her foot.

'I knew I'd find you here.'

Paige startled a little as she looked up to see Nat beaming at her from the open doorway.

'Hi.' She smiled back, gesturing for her friend to enter.

'Oh, sorry,' Nat whispered, plonking herself in the chair opposite. 'I didn't realise you were on the phone.'

'It's okay. I'm on hold. What's up? You look like you just won a million bucks.'

Nat grinned. 'Better. I'm—'

Paige held a finger up as the receptionist came on the other end. 'Just a sec,' she said apologetically. 'Hi, yes, my name's Paige Donald. I was wondering if Dr Mantara could squeeze me in this afternoon?'

Paige listened as the receptionist explained it was impossible and tried not to scream her frustration down the phone. There was no point in shooting the messenger. She took an early morning appointment the next day instead and hung up.

Nat crinkled her brow. 'Everything okay?'

Paige sighed. 'I don't know.' She looked at her friend. They'd been close during school but life had pulled them apart again until the last few years. Paige just hadn't had the time or an excess of emotional energy for the type of friendship most women valued. She didn't realise how isolated she'd become until right now as the urge to unburden took her by surprise.

'I think…' She hesitated, unused to sharing such private matters. 'I think I have a UTI.'

'Okay.' Nat leaned forward, placing her elbows on the desk. 'Why don't you start at the beginning?'

Paige told her about the day and the inconvenient frequency symptoms. 'It has to be a UTI, right?'

Nat regarded her for a few moments. 'You're not…? Could you be…pregnant?'

It took a few seconds for Paige to compute what her friend had said. And she laughed. 'Don't be ridiculous,' she dismissed. And then she sobered as a cold hand clutched at her gut. No way. She couldn't be. Surely?

Nat watched a procession of emotions march across her friend's face. 'Are you sure? I thought you and Valentino might be getting—'

'Quite sure,' Paige interrupted, her heart booming like church bells in her chest.

Nat didn't think Paige looked overly convinced. She reached into her handbag. 'I just happen to have an extra one of these.' She placed a packaged pregnancy test on the desk and pushed it towards Paige.

Paige looked at it like it was a venomous snake. She could not be pregnant. Could not. An image rose unbidden in her mind. Daisy's tiny white coffin covered in pale pink roses.

Even now it had the power to paralyse her.

'You know it's the first thing the GP's going to do anyway,' Nat murmured. 'Might as well save her the effort.'

Paige nodded, knowing Nat was right. She looked at the test again, a sudden thought occurring to her. 'Just happen to have this huh?'

Nat shrugged. 'I bought one of those two-in-ones… in case.'

Paige could tell from her friend's face that she'd already used the first one and was trying really hard to be sensitive to Paige's situation in the face of her own good news. 'Does this mean congratulations are in order?'

Nat nodded and then grinned. 'You're the first one to know.'

Paige grinned back, even though inside she felt bleaker than a Bronte moor. 'That's fabulous, Nat.' She leaned forward and gave her friend a big hug. 'Alessandro and Juliano will be over the moon.'

'They'll be ecstatic,' Nat agreed. 'I've been trying to get hold of Alessandro for the last two hours but he's not answering. I just had to tell someone.'

Paige smiled. 'I feel honoured.'

They chatted for the next few minutes about due dates and morning sickness until Nat's phone beeped with a message from Alessandro. 'He's at home.'

'Well, what are you waiting for? Off you go,' Paige teased. When Nat hesitated she said, 'I mean it, go. I'll be fine.'

Nat stood. 'You will do the test, won't you?'

Paige eyeballed it, remembering the last time she'd done a pregnancy test. The joy. The hope. She looked away. 'Yes.'

'I'm going to ring in the morning and check on you.'

Paige rolled her eyes. 'Yes, ma'am.'

Nat leaned down and gave her friend a quick squeeze. 'I'll see you tomorrow.'

The room seemed preternaturally quiet after Nat left. There was just Paige and the test and her heart beat ticking loudly in the silence like the doomsday clock.

Her fingers trembled as she picked it up and turned it over and over. She couldn't do pregnant again. After Daisy had died she'd vowed to never make herself vulnerable like that again. She couldn't stand nine months of living on the edge, being paranoid about things going wrong, demanding scans every week, thinking the worst should there be no foetal movements for a minute, an hour, a day.

Giving birth in a haze of anxiety, constantly testing the baby's hearing, driving herself insane at the slightest sniffle.

Oh, God. What if it was twins again?

And what about McKenzie? Her child, the one she already had, needed her. There was no time for another. Certainly not for two. There was no spare time to give at all.

She just couldn't do it again.

'Are you going to take that or just stare at it?'

Paige didn't have to look up to know Valentino was standing there. He sounded annoyed.

He could get in line.

'I have a UTI,' she said, raising her face defiantly.

Even glowering at her from the doorway he looked magnificent and her breath caught in her throat. His hair was all messy from the cap and his top two buttons were undone. In another time and place, having his baby would have made her very happy indeed.

'Is that why you kept leaving the theatre today?'

'Yes,' she said testily.

'So why bother with that?'

She shrugged. 'Just pre-empting my GP.'

Valentino's heart beat a crazy tattoo in his chest. What if she was pregnant? What if his baby was already growing inside her? 'What if it's positive?'

Paige felt her stress levels rise a notch. 'It won't be.'

'What if it is?' he insisted.

'It isn't.'

Valentino wanted to shake her. Years ago he'd known briefly what it was like to have created life before it had been snatched away. He was surprised now at how fiercely he still wanted it. 'So go and prove me wrong.'

Paige swallowed. She should. She knew she should. But at least here and now, with the test tucked safely away in its packaging, she could believe in her denial. Once it was out, once the test had been done, it became a whole different proposition.

She stood. 'Fine.' It had been twenty minutes since she had last gone and the urge had returned with a vengeance. May as well get it over and done with. Then at least she could discount pregnancy and get on with having the right tests done.

Valentino stood his ground as she brushed by. He would not be shut out the second time around. 'I'll wait in the lounge.'

Paige's legs felt like wet noodles as she made her way through the lounge area to the staff toilet. Her hands shook as she undid the packaging and it took her several attempts before she was able to liberate it. Between her nerveless fingers and the vibrations of her heartbeat she was frightened she was going to drop the damn thing in the loo!

She doubted very much that Valentino understood the potential impact of this test. How could a footloose, fancy-free, playboy bachelor understand the full implications? For him it was no doubt a test of his virility. Proof of his manliness.

But for her? It was a whole different proposition.

Still, regardless of that, it did need to be done so she took a deep breath and managed to eke out enough urine to do the test.

And even before the little plus appeared somewhere inside she knew.

'Well?' Valentino asked as she appeared back in the open lounge area.

Paige held up the test, barely keeping upright as the foundations of her world crashed all round her. 'It's positive.'

Valentino stared at the pink plus sign. It was a full minute before the information sank in. He was going to be a father. He smiled. And then he grinned. 'This is the best news I've ever heard.'

Paige wasn't similarly overcome. In fact, a huge block of emotion built in her chest till she thought she was going to pass out from the pressure of it. It stung her eyes and prickled in her nose. She sucked in a breath. 'No, Valentino, it's not. This is the worst possible news. You have no idea.'

And she burst into tears.

CHAPTER SIX

WHATEVER Valentino had been expecting it hadn't been this and confronted with her emotional state, he felt at a loss. 'Hey,' he crooned, stepping forward and putting his arm around her shoulders.

Paige shrugged his arm away and moved back. 'Don't touch me,' she half snapped, half sobbed as she wiped at her face with the heels of her palms. 'That's what got us into this mess in the first place.'

'It's not a mess, Paige,' Valentino said gently. 'I'm really okay with this.'

Paige felt a bubble of hysteria rise in her throat to join the mix of other emotions. 'How lovely,' she said sarcastically.

'I'm just saying—'

'Do me a favour,' she interrupted. 'Don't say anything, okay?'

Valentino wisely followed her advice, standing silently, his fists curled by his sides while tears poured down her face. She was in shock. She needed a little time to wrap her head around it. He understood that. But as far as he was concerned, he'd been primed for this moment for a long time. Ever since his ex-fiancée had come into his hospital half-dead from a botched backyard abortion.

Yes, since then he'd taken precautions to avoid it but whether it was his Italian pride or his legendary uncle status, he'd always known deep down that he wanted to be a father.

And he would move heaven and earth to make sure this child, his child, had everything it ever wanted.

Paige didn't know what to do with herself. Valentino had sat on one of the lounge chairs and was regarding her with his steady brown gaze. 'How can you be so calm?' she demanded. Her cheeks felt hot and she knew she must look a mess. Her nose was running and her face was no doubt an ugly, blotchy mess.

Valentino shrugged. 'I don't see the point in hysteria.'

Oh, really? As far as she was concerned, this was precisely the moment for hysteria. 'Why?' she asked, raking her hands through her hair. 'Why did you have to come along and ruin everything? I was perfectly happy the way I was.'

Valentino was prepared to talk about it, he was even prepared to argue and to cope with more tears, but he wouldn't sit here and listen to her lie to herself. 'I think we both know that's not true.'

Paige choked on a sob. What did he know about her life? 'Are you calling me a liar?'

'I'm just calling it like I see it, Paige.'

Paige's lips twisted into a bitter grimace. 'Oh? And what do you see? This should be interesting.'

'I see a woman whose world was torn apart. One who's going through the motions but can't get any enjoyment out of life. I see someone who's physically and emotionally starving.'

Paige shied away from the truth that resonated in his words. 'I'm eating,' she said, completely exasperated.

'Great. So your stomach is full but what fills your emotional well, Paige?'

'That doesn't matter,' she dismissed.

Valentino snorted. 'Of course it does.'

'Well, what fills yours, then, Valentino?'

'Vivaldi.' It was sterner than he had meant it to come out but her stonewalling was frustrating in the extreme. He continued in a gentler tone. 'A letter from my mother. The first time a patient hears sound. Children laughing. Bruschetta. The way a woman's waist curves out to her hip. *Swan Lake.*'

Hell, did he think she had time for ballet? 'What? No raindrops on roses?'

'Paige.' This was no time for deflection. 'The point is I can take enjoyment from the world around me. When was the last time you did that? When was the last time you rejoiced in being alive?'

Paige fleetingly thought about those few seconds of dread that she woke with every morning and quickly pushed them aside.

'Oh, for crying out loud,' she snapped. 'I don't have time to get my emotional well filled.' She suddenly felt overwhelmed by everything and sat in the lounge opposite Valentino. 'I'm the sole parent to a high-needs child. I certainly don't have time for another baby. That wouldn't be fair to McKenzie.'

'You don't think McKenzie would like a brother or a sister?'

Paige rubbed her brow. 'I'm sure she would. I'm also pretty sure she'd like a unicorn. Unfortunately she doesn't get a say.'

Valentino chuckled but, as he had just stated, she didn't find any joy in it. She turned beseeching eyes on him. 'I'm tired, Valentino.'

'I'll be here. I'll help.'

Her gaze turned quickly incredulous. How long would it take an Italian playboy surgeon with an international reputation to grow tired of playing house in little old Brisbane? She hardened her heart to his pretty words. Arnie had also promised he'd help. Promised he'd be here until death parted them.

Obviously he'd taken Daisy's death as a literal translation. Their daughter hadn't even been in the ground a week when he'd left for good. She couldn't go through that kind of heartbreak again. She just couldn't.

'And when London calls? When Harry gets back?'

Valentino hadn't thought that far ahead. 'Then you come with me.'

Paige felt the broken edges of her heart grate together. 'No, Valentino. I won't. This is my home. It's McKenzie's home. And whether you like it or not, we are a package deal. I'm not going to uproot her when she has years of therapy left.'

'They do have speech pathologists in other parts of the world.'

Of course they did but Paige had vowed never to blindly follow a man again, like she had Arnie. 'She trusts the St Auburn's team. Has built a relationship with them.'

He shrugged. 'Children adapt.'

Paige glared at him. Spoken like a true egotist, used only to looking after himself. Not a responsible father who put the needs of a child first. 'So let me get this straight. You want me to up sticks and follow you around the world with your child without any mention of us? Of our relationship? Do you even love me, Valentino?'

Valentino could see the stormy uncertainty in her gaze, the earnestness. He looked away. Love? *Dio!* He was too busy trying to come to terms with becoming a father. 'I don't think that's relevant.'

Paige's head spun at his quick dismissal of the fundamental human emotion. 'How is it not relevant, Valentino? Do you expect me to follow you around like a puppy dog, hoping you can squeeze your child in between your work and dating catwalk models?'

Valentino stood, the scorn in her voice stabbing like a stiletto between his ribs. '*Dio!* No, I have more respect for you than that. We would marry, of course.'

Paige blinked up at him. If that was a proposal, it sucked big time. Not to mention it was utter insanity. 'What?'

He hadn't given any of this much thought but now it was out there he knew it was the right thing to do. 'We'll get married.'

'You just told me that love wasn't relevant and now you want to marry me?' Try as she may, Paige couldn't rid her voice of its high squeaky quality.

It had been a long time since Valentino had thought about love. About those three little words. But he did remember how callously they could be used. How empty they could be. 'Did you love your husband?'

Paige frowned. 'Yes. Of course.'

'How'd that work out for you?'

Paige gasped. If her legs had been feeling remotely solid, she would have stood up and slapped his face.

Valentino could see he'd shocked her. Hurt her. He hadn't meant to be so insensitive. He sat. 'I'm sorry, that was unthinking of me.'

She was sitting hunched forward in her chair and he reached across the space between them to squeeze her arm but Paige moved back out of his reach.

'Yes, it was.'

Valentino regarded her solemnly for a few moments. 'I don't have all the answers yet, Paige. I'm just saying we can work them out. We have time.'

Except the thought of going through it all again, of growing a baby inside, loving it, wanting it, was just too much for her to bear. Her head throbbed in unison with her heart. It was just all too overwhelming.

She stood. 'I can't think straight any more. I have to get home. Mum will be wondering where I am.'

Valentino nodded. 'Of course. Will you tell them about the baby?'

Paige frowned, her mind too full to think straight. 'Of course. Eventually.'

She shuffled her feet awkwardly for a moment. Valentino's head was downcast. This had no doubt thrown a huge spanner into the works for him too. And even though he'd just made the most preposterous suggestion she'd ever heard, she kind of got where it came from. This whole thing was completely unexpected.

She had the strangest urge to gather him in close and lay his cheek against her belly where their baby grew. Instead, she brushed past him with a quiet 'Goodnight'.

Valentino grabbed her hand as she went by. She looked down at him and he fixed her with imploring eyes. 'You won't do anything...rash, will you?'

His meaning was clear and her first reaction was anger. Did he seriously think she would go off behind his back and terminate his baby? Or that she'd go off riding a wild bronco or throw herself off a cliff with only a bungee cord around her ankle? But there was a plea in his gaze that reached right inside her gut and she realised he was as vulnerable, as unsure as she. He had as much at stake as she did.

It seemed natural then to follow through on her earlier impulse and move closer. She buried her hand in his hair and urged his cheek against her stomach.

'Of course not. I won't do anything without talking to you first.'

Valentino shut his eyes as her fingers sifted through his hair and her aroma filled his senses. Her words were utterly sincere and he didn't doubt her. 'Thank you,' he murmured, turning his face to press a kiss against her belly where his child nestled.

Paige shut her eyes as the innocent gesture constricted her throat and breathed fire into her belly. She wished she could give him what he wanted. But what about when it conflicted with what she wanted?

What about her?

'I need time to think. I have to go,' she said, wriggling out of his hold and striding away without looking back.

After a fitful sleep, Paige woke the next morning with only the craving to eat everything in her pantry trumping the dire urge to empty her bladder. She couldn't remember the last time she'd woken with biological matters taking such urgent precedence.

Usually she had to fight herself out of a thick shroud of grief that seemed to pounce in her sleep, making her limbs weak and dampening her mood, steeling herself to face the day for McKenzie's sake. But this morning she was so hungry none of that registered. She would have eaten the sheets had she been tied to the bed.

The devastating fact of her pregnancy, the thing that had had her tossing and turning all night, seemed to pale in comparison to her hunger. She felt like a grizzly bear coming awake after a long winter's hibernation.

The doorbell rang as Paige passed it and she checked her watch. Seven-thirty. A little early for her parents to be here. McKenzie, unusually, was still sound asleep. Paige had checked on her twice already.

She opened the door to find Valentino standing there. He looked good, even for someone with bloodshot eyes and hair that appeared to have been raked all night. It was on the tip of her tongue to tell him to leave then she spied the brown bakery bag under his arm at the same time a waft of yeasty goodness reached her nose.

'Oh, God,' she said, grabbing the bag, her mouth watering already. 'Come in,' she ordered, turning on her heel as she opened the bag and the warm sweet smell of freshly baked croissants hit her olfactory system.

Valentino blinked as Paige disappeared as quickly as she had appeared. He looked at the space where his offering had been and was now gone. He'd been expecting many things this morning. More tears. More anger. Recriminations.

Certainly not this.

Hunger was a good sign, yes?

He found her in the kitchen, tearing chunks off a croissant and stuffing them into her mouth. She was making short work of it. It was compelling viewing as flakes of pastry stuck to her lips and she made little noises of pleasure at the back of her throat as each morsel hit her taste buds.

In fact, he was rather turned on.

When Paige opened her eyes Valentino was the first thing she saw, leaning casually in her doorway. She wasn't sure if it was the morning light or the sugar rush but he looked pretty good there.

'Do you own anything that's not ten sizes too big?' he mused.

'Sit.' She gestured to the stool opposite, ignoring him as she stuffed the last piece of her croissant into her mouth. She turned and retrieved some plates from the cupboard behind her and placed a croissant on each one, pushing his towards him.

She nodded at the side counter. 'Coffee percolator if you want one.'

Valentino would rather never drink coffee again than settle for the stuff that Australians euphemistically called coffee. 'Not even if I was dying,' he said dryly.

Paige laughed. She actually laughed at the disdain on his face. 'Snob.' And then she tore some off her second croissant and devoured it. 'God, this is so-o-o good,' she sighed, licking her fingers.

Valentino temporarily lost his train of thought. Watching her eat was gastronomic pornography. 'Your appetite has returned, I see.'

She nodded. 'I'm so-o-o hungry. I'd forgotten how good things taste,' she said around another mouthful.

'Pleased I could be of service.' He made a mental note to bring a wider array of tempting goodies every time he called in. Which hopefully would be often.

Valentino watched her choose a third croissant, bringing it to her lips, opening her mouth but stopping before she took the first bite. 'Oh, I'm sorry. This is yours,' she said, placing it back on top of the bag.

Valentino chuckled. 'Take it.'

'No, no.' Paige shook her head even as the flaky pastry called to her like a mermaid luring sailors onto the rocks.

He picked it up and held it out. 'I wouldn't dream of depriving you, *bella*.'

Paige winced and hesitated. 'I'm being a pig, aren't I?'

Valentino shook his head. 'I could watch you eat all day,' he murmured, and passed the croissant slowly beneath her nose. 'Besides, you're eating for two now, remember?'

Paige made a grab for the pastry on his second pass. Not even the reminder of her predicament, their predicament, overrode her stomach's demands. Maybe the decision she'd come to in the wee small hours made everything a little easier.

She sank her teeth in, the flakes of soft, velvety pastry melting as they hit her tongue. 'Mmm,' she sighed.

Valentino waited until she finished, not wanting it to end but knowing they had things to discuss. 'We need to talk.' He pulled a tissue out of the box on the counter top and passed it to her, knowing he wasn't going to be able to concentrate with delicate flakes clinging to her gorgeous mouth.

'Sorry,' she apologised, licking at her lips, desperately playing for time now her stomach was satisfied. What had seemed thoroughly reasonable at 3 a.m. didn't seem so reasonable with Valentino sitting in her kitchen. 'I bet it's everywhere.'

Valentino almost groaned as her pink tongue ran back and forth very thoroughly over her lips, picking up stray flakes. Then she dabbed at her mouth with the tissue like a proper society matron. Like she hadn't just done a good impression of the cookie monster or licked her lips like a porn star.

'So,' he said, trying to wrangle his thoughts and the ruckus in his underpants back under control. 'The baby.

You said you needed time to think. I don't know about you but I've thought of little else since yesterday afternoon.'

Paige nodded. This was it. She only hoped he understood. 'I can't have this baby, Valentino. I just can't.' She held up her hand as he opened his mouth to protest. 'Please, just hear me out.' She shifted off the stool. 'I want to show you something.'

Valentino followed Paige into the lounge room, his anger simmering. If she thought he would sit by and let her decide the outcome for their baby then she was sorely mistaken. Despite evidence to the contrary only a minute ago, he felt so impotent. He would not let another woman take from him what was also his.

'Sit down.'

He sat and watched her, his thoughts swirling and brooding inside like a gathering storm. She opened a cupboard beneath some bookshelves and pulled out what appeared to be a photo album. She stood for a moment, running her forefinger over the front cover before turning back towards him and sitting down next to him.

Paige passed him the album, her hands trembling. Her eyes locked with his. Her fingers kept hold of the object, lingering, reluctant to surrender it even when she knew it would help him to understand.

'I've never shown this to anyone before.'

Valentino nodded. He could see her qualms swirling like encroaching fog in her big grey eyes and he felt her resistance when he tried to take the album from her. He could see the struggle and what it took for her to finally release it to him.

'I am honoured,' he murmured.

His gaze fell on the window cut out of the cover. It was a close-up of a tiny baby, eyes closed, crisscrossed with tubes and wires. The only way to even tell its sex was from the tiny pink knitted cap that fitted snugly over its head. The little girl was clasping an adult finger in the foreground. It dwarfed the little babe's arm, giving true perspective to its size.

'This is Daisy, yes?'

Paige nodded. 'Yes.'

Valentino hesitated, even though she'd yielded the album to him. 'May I?'

Paige took a deep breath and nodded. Valentino opened the cover slowly, as if he'd just been handed an incredibly old parchment, and she was touched by his reverence.

Her gaze fell to the pages. There, first up, was a picture of Daisy at four hours old. And three years rushed out at her, sucking her straight back into the tumult. The anguish.

'They were twenty-seven-weekers, yes?'

Paige nodded as he continued his reverent journey through the album. 'Daisy was nine hundred grams. McKenzie was twelve hundred.'

Ah. That explained a lot. Premature babies born under one kilo had the odds truly stacked against them.

'It's a beautiful album,' he commented as each picture chronicled Daisy's battle and ever-increasing medical support. The pages were pale pink and decorated with pretty stickers, silky ribbons and baby-themed cut-outs. Every effort had been made to present Daisy as a baby, a precious gift, cherished and loved.

'My mother made the album for me after…'

Valentino didn't push her to complete the sentence. 'It's a good idea. She obviously took a great deal of care with it.'

Paige nodded. 'Mum's very good at craftwork. She does all her own stationery and cards.'

Valentino flipped the pages over, taking great care to linger over each photo with the reverence it deserved. Towards the end they became more medicalised. There were more tubes than baby.

'She had several chest tubes, I see.'

'She kept blowing pneumothoraxes towards the end. Her chronic neonatal lung disease was so bad she didn't respond to any treatment and they just couldn't ventilate her.'

Valentino didn't say anything. What was there to say? It must have been agony to watch. In fact, it was written all over Paige's face in the photos. The album wasn't just a timeline of Daisy's life but a startling map of Paige's grief.

'They withdrew treatment?'

'Yes. She'd suffered so much.' Paige reached out and traced Daisy's face with her forefinger. 'We couldn't ask any more of her.'

The 'we' soon became evident as Valentino turned to the second last page. A photo of a blond man looking down at Daisy, his hand resting against her ever-present woollen cap, jumped out at him. 'Your husband?'

Paige nodded. 'Arnie.'

'He…left?'

'Two days after Daisy's funeral.'

Valentino gripped the edges of the album. How could he do that? How could he walk away from his grieving wife and his other child? What kind of a man did that? 'Do you have contact with him? Does McKenzie see him?'

Was that one of the other factors that Paige had to consider? Was she still carrying a candle for him? The thought struck deep in Valentino's chest. Surely not?

Paige snorted. 'The only correspondence I've had from Arnie since the day I begged him not to leave me has been through his lawyer when the divorce papers arrived.'

Her voice was laced with bitterness and Valentino knew without a shadow of a doubt that it was Arnie he had to thank for Paige's less than flattering opinion of men, the brick wall around her heart. But at least she seemed well and truly over him.

Valentino flipped to the last page. He felt Paige tense beside him and he could see why. It was a very raw photo, difficult to even look at without feeling as if he had intruded on something truly intimate. A snapshot full of utter human misery. Painfully private.

Paige was holding a swaddled Daisy. She was free of all her tubes, her eyes swollen and closed, pink cap pulled snugly over her head. Her mouth was a straight line, the lips colourless, her skin deathly pale. The caption in stickers read 'Rest In Peace Our Precious Daisy'.

Paige was crying in the photograph as she looked down at her daughter with such anguish, clearly distressed. Like she'd give anything in that moment to bring her daughter back. Trade places even. The look said, Don't go, I haven't had the chance to get to know you yet.

Completely desolate was a good description and Valentino felt it right to his very soul.

'She was just too little,' Paige whispered. It had been a couple of years since she'd seen this photo. Tears burned at the backs of her eyes and then welled up and spilled over.

'She fought the good fight,' Valentino murmured.

'She did. She fought for so long.'

Valentino heard the sob catch in her throat and put his arm around her, tucking her head against his shoulder.

He closed the album and let Paige cry until her tears ran out.

Paige wasn't sure how much time had elapsed when she pulled away from him. She was just grateful he'd let her cry. He hadn't tried to tell her not to upset herself or be brave for McKenzie, as Arnie had. He'd just been there.

She used her baggy sleeve to dry her face. 'Do you see why I can't go through another pregnancy? I can't lose another child, Valentino.'

Valentino knew he had to tread carefully here. That just because Paige's fears weren't necessarily rational, it didn't mean they weren't real to her. 'I understand why you don't want to be emotionally vulnerable again. You've been through a lot in the last few years.'

Paige nodded, pleased to see he understood. 'Don't you see?' she reasoned. 'If there is no baby then there's no chance of what happened to the twins happening again.'

Valentino took her hand. 'But there is a baby, Paige.

Do you think terminating a pregnancy doesn't count as losing a child?'

'It's…it's different,' she said defensively.

'No, it's not.'

Paige looked at him sharply. Just when she'd thought he understood. 'Is this a religious thing?'

Valentino's brow crinkled. 'What?'

'You're Italian. I know it's frowned on there…'

Valentino was trying to hold onto his temper but it was fraying rapidly. 'This has nothing to do with religion. It's my child, Paige. My. Child. I have rights too and if you think I'm going to allow you to terminate this pregnancy, you're very wrong.'

Paige was surprised to feel the depth of his convictions blast towards her. The vehemence in his speech. The fierce light burning in his gaze. But it didn't mean he could dictate to her.

'Why?' she demanded. 'Why do you care so much? This whole thing smacks of commitment, of long term. I'd have thought you'd be running a mile.'

Valentino knew her assessment was justified but it stung anyway. He stood and strode to the glass doors that overlooked the deck.

'You thought wrong.'

CHAPTER SEVEN

PAIGE flinched at the steel in Valentino's voice. But as he continued to stare out of her windows, his hands buried in his pockets, she sensed there was more to his insistence then she knew.

'Is there something you're not telling me?'

Valentino could hear his heartbeat pounding like surf in his head. He hadn't spoken her name in years. But if ever there was a time to open up, this was it. Paige had just shared a part of her life that was intensely private. Maybe it was time to share his?

'There was a woman.' His voice was husky and he cleared it. 'A long time ago.'

Paige stilled. Ah. 'I see.'

Valentino turned. Where did he even start? 'We were in love. Or at least I thought we were. I was first year out, an intern, back home. She was a fashion design student. She was…beautiful.'

It was a surprise how much it hurt to hear him talk about a woman in such hushed, awed tones. And even though he was looking at her, Paige knew he'd gone somewhere far away.

'She was twenty-one and she had all these curves and this gorgeous long hair…'

Valentino stopped and Paige didn't need to join the dots to know the woman must have been a stunner. She suddenly felt plain and unattractive with her short hair and angular frame.

What had Valentino seen in her?

'I was completely besotted. I proposed within two months and she leapt at it. Bought her this magnificent rock because she just had to have it. We went to lots of parties, made the society pages. She bragged about marrying a doctor to all her friends and revelled in the kudos.'

He paused for breath and Paige spoke for the first time. 'What was her name?'

Valentino fought his way back from the past and Paige slowly came into focus. 'Daniella.'

Once even the mention of the name had sent him a little crazy but he was surprised at how unaffected he felt, standing here today.

What on earth had he seen in her? Looking at Paige now, an intriguing woman with depth and layers, he just couldn't figure it out. Daniella had been terribly superficial. Yes, she'd been young but all she'd cared about had been clothes and shoes and the trendy new bars in town. He could admit now that conversation had been terribly dull. He'd just been too in lust to see it.

'Then I took her to meet my parents. The whole sign-language thing freaked her out, I think. And when I started to talk about setting a date and planning a family, she ran a mile. She had a career and a social life. How could she possibly fit into her designer wardrobe or drink champagne at glamorous balls with swollen feet and no waist? What if we had a deaf child?'

Paige heard the bitter edge to his voice. 'Ah.'

Valentino nodded. 'I was devastated.'

'Of course. First love is always the hardest.'

Despite having dated on and off throughout her twenties, Arnie had been her first love. She'd fallen for him hard and married him in a rush. His desertion when she'd needed him most had cut deep.

As, obviously, had Daniella's. Suddenly his playboy rebound love-life made sense. He'd evidently been trying to forget Daniella's callousness. Who was she to judge how he dealt with his loss? Just because she'd withdrawn completely, it didn't mean it was the right way to cope.

Was there a book of etiquette somewhere that explained how you were supposed to act when your whole world fell apart?

Valentino's mouth compressed into a tight line. 'There's more.' He hesitated. How did he say something he'd never truly voiced to anyone before? 'Six weeks after we broke up I was working night shift in Emergency when Daniella was rushed through the doors. She was haemorrhaging heavily. She'd had a back-street abortion.'

Paige gasped. She hadn't expected that. 'Oh, Valentino.'

She got to her feet, crossed the short space between them and placed her hand on his arm. 'I'm so sorry.'

He captured her gaze. 'She didn't tell me she was pregnant. She didn't ask me for help or bother to find out what I wanted. She just went and took my child from me.'

She closed her eyes against the anguish she saw in Valentino's. She knew how it felt to have a child taken from you. No wonder he'd been so vehement with her. It must be like Daniella all over again. 'You wanted to keep the baby?'

Valentino gave her a hard look. 'I wanted the choice. I wanted to be consulted. Included.'

Paige nodded. 'That was wrong of her. To act without consulting you.'

'Damn right.'

'She was young and scared,' Paige said gently.

'So was I,' he said. 'But I'm not now.'

Paige sighed and returned to the lounge. She raised pleading eyes to him. 'Valentino, please don't make this more difficult for me than it already is.'

'You want me to make it easy for you? I won't.'

He strode towards her, dropping to his knees beside her. He grabbed her hand and pressed it to her belly. 'Feel that. Inside there is our baby. He lives and he grows. He has a heartbeat and every right to be born. He's going to have my dark wavy hair and your beautiful grey eyes and he's going to be healthy and perfect and we're going to love him.'

Paige shook her head from side to side. Damn him. It was ridiculous to think she could feel the baby move but she could have sworn tiny flutters danced beneath their joined hands. And suddenly she could picture him.

Him! For crying out loud!

Just as Valentino had described him. Perfect in every way. A unique blend of both of them.

And she knew she couldn't do it. Not to Valentino. Or herself. Or the baby. A baby she already loved more than life itself. As she had loved Daisy and McKenzie from the second she'd known about them. Who was she kidding? She could no more deny this tiny life growing inside her than fly to the moon.

And looking at Valentino's tormented face, she knew she couldn't hurt him either. Not like that. Not like Daniella had.

Her gaze fell on the album beside her and she touched Daisy's cheek with heart-breaking reverence. 'Chances of delivering early again increase in subsequent pregnancies.' She glanced at Valentino with huge eyes. 'I'm scared,' she whispered.

'Don't be. I'm not going to let anything happen to our baby.'

And for a crazy moment she believed him.

The next day Valentino arrived on her doorstep, bearing freshly baked blueberry muffins. And an engagement ring.

'Dr Valentino!'

'Well, good morning, young lady.' Valentino crouched down, signing as he spoke. He could just make out the external component of the implant attached to the side of her head and mostly hidden by her gorgeous curls. She was wearing a pink tutu and fairy wings, which looked even sweeter on her diminutive frame.

'*Osservate molto abbastanza oggi.*' Although he spoke in Italian he signed in English so she knew she was looking very pretty today.

'We're having breakfast,' McKenzie signed with a flourish.

'That's good.' Valentino grinned. He opened the bag and let McKenzie peek inside. 'I brought muffins.'

'McKenzie, darling?'

Valentino stood as an unfamiliar voice came closer. It sounded older. Paige was obviously not alone.

'Oh. Hello, there.'

An older woman with Paige's big grey eyes blinked curiously at him. He recognised her from the photo on the television. 'Hi. I'm Valentino,' he said, holding out his hand.

'Oh, yes.' Paige's mother shook his hand. 'You're the surgeon who took over from Harry. You did McKenzie's surgery.'

Valentino smiled. 'Yes.' McKenzie slipped her hand into his and he watched as the older woman's shrewd gaze followed the movement.

'I didn't realise you made house calls?'

Valentino saw the teasing sparkle in her eyes and chuckled. 'Only for my special patients,' he said, grinning down at McKenzie and signing for her benefit.

'I'm Adele, Paige's mother.'

'Very pleased to meet you.'

And he was. Adele was a fine-looking woman. Tall, like her daughter, she'd aged well with graceful laughter lines around her eyes and mouth. But what struck him the most was her aura of contentment. Adele obviously lived well and laughed a lot. She looked healthy and robust and mischief danced in her eyes. She reminded him of his own mother.

'Would you care to join us for breakfast?'

Valentino held up the bakery packet, pleased to have bought a few extras. 'I brought muffins.'

'I'm sure they'll be welcome. My daughter seems to have found her appetite at last.'

She gave him a speculative look before turning on her heel, and Valentino smiled as he and McKenzie followed her.

'Look who I found lurking in the doorway,' Adele announced as she stepped onto the deck.

An older man looked up from several newspapers he appeared to be reading at once. He looked at Valentino over the top of bifocal glasses with a startled expression. Paige looked up from buttering the last slice of toast.

'Valentino!'

She wanted to say this really had to stop but he looked all sexy in his casual chinos and open-necked shirt and infinitely male and his dimples screamed lazy Sunday morning.

But this really had to stop.

Adele could see the indecision on her daughter's face. 'He brought muffins,' she said, digging Valentino in the ribs.

Valentino smiled to himself and held out the bag

exactly as Adele had no doubt hoped he would. 'Blueberry,' he said. 'Warm. Just out of the oven.'

Paige relented. How could she still be hungry after an omelette stuffed with mushrooms, cheese and bacon and three pieces of toast? 'My favourite.'

Adele relieved him of the packet, placing it in the centre of the table, and walked around to the empty chair beside Paige and pulled it out for him. 'Sit here, Valentino.'

As a well-adjusted Italian male, Valentino had a healthy respect for mothers and wasn't about to argue with one who would hopefully soon be his mother-in-law. But before he sat he stretched his hand across the table towards the man he assumed was Paige's father.

'Hello, sir. I'm Valentino Lombardi. Pleased to meet you.'

Paige's father half stood as he accepted Valentino's hand in a firm, brief shake. 'McKenzie's surgeon? Don Eden.' He looked over his glasses at his wife as he re-claimed his seat, speculation in his gaze. 'Didn't realise you blokes made house calls.'

Valentino grinned as Adele winked at him. 'Coffee?'

'Valentino would rather eat dirt then drink our heathen colonial coffee,' Paige said around a mouthful of muffin. 'Is that a fair summation?'

Valentino chuckled. She had crumbs on her lips and it was most distracting. It was sexy, watching her eat with such gusto. He wondered how she'd look eating something gooey, like ice cream. In bed. With no clothes on. 'More than fair.'

'Oh, I don't blame you,' Adele said. 'Nicest coffee we ever had was in Italy, wasn't it, darling? Where are you from exactly?' she asked.

They chatted for half an hour about Italy and travelling and McKenzie's implant. Not that Paige contributed much. After eating two muffins she dropped her head back against her chair and shut her eyes, letting the morning sunshine warm her skin.

She didn't want to encourage him, she didn't want him too cosy with her family. Just because she'd agreed not to do anything rash, it didn't mean they were one big happy family.

Despite his assurances of support, Paige had been burnt before.

It was pleasant conversation but Valentino was charming her parents and it was strangely irritating. As good as he was to look at, as amazing as he smelled this morning—like bakery and sunshine—she wished he would just go.

Valentino found his attention drifting as he chatted with Adele and Don. He was hyper-aware of Paige beside him all loose and relaxed in her chair. She was wearing her usual baggy clothes but whether it was the angle of her body or this particular view he couldn't help but notice how fuller her breasts seemed. How they formed two firm, high mounds against the thin fabric of her shirt and bounced when she shifted in the chair.

He wanted to nuzzle her neck, let his hand drift to one of those very enticing mounds.

Dio!

He came here for one thing and one thing only. He

rose, needing desperately to get away and get his mind back on the game plan. 'Excuse me for a moment.' Valentino stood. 'Paige, your bathroom?'

Paige gave him directions and, despite wanting him to leave only seconds ago, she suddenly felt bereft without him. She steeled herself for the grilling she knew was to come.

Her mother went first. 'I like him.'

'You don't know him.'

'I'd known Arnie for two minutes and knew I didn't like him.'

Touché. She glanced at her father smiling at her mother, his dimples blazing. 'You've always been a sucker for men with dimples.'

Adele ignored him and looked at her daughter. 'So have you, darling.'

Had she? When she looked back over her life prior to Arnie the few boyfriends she'd had had indeed all been blessed with dimples. 'Dimples do not maketh the man,' Paige grumbled.

Adele smiled at her husband. 'I would have to disagree with you there.'

Paige shook her head, humbled as ever by her parents' enduring love and affection for each other. 'Well, you would.'

'I'm just saying that I think he's good for you.' Adele reached across the table and squeezed her daughter's hand. 'Isn't it about time you declared a truce on the men of the world? They're not all like Arnie, darling.'

Paige wondered how her parents would feel if they

knew that this Italian Lothario they were so enamoured with had impregnated their daughter. Neither of her parents were keen for her to have any more children given what had happened with the twins.

Before she could speak, Valentino's voice drifted out to them and three pairs of eyes sought him out. He'd stopped to talk to McKenzie.

McKenzie had grown bored quickly with the adult conversation and had asked for 'Wigga' and Paige, who didn't like her watching too much television, hadn't been able to refuse. Hearing her daughter say actual words was sweeter than the sweetest music in the world and seeing her dance now she could actually hear the music was endlessly thrilling.

They watched as Valentino took McKenzie's hands and danced around with her. McKenzie giggled as he lifted her off the floor and twirled her round, his dark hair almost black compared to her lighter hues. She clapped as he put her down and said, 'Again.' And Valentino complied, his easy laughter rich and deep.

Laughter you could drown in.

And her broken, fractured, battered, stomped-on heart just about melted in her chest.

'Oh, my,' Adele said, her hand fluttering to her chest.

Paige dragged her gaze away from the endearing sight of Valentino—a large, virile, Italian man his hands dwarfing McKenzie's torso—twirling her daughter—a little pink fairy girl—round and round. It was exceedingly sexy.

She blasted her mother with an impatient glare. So

he was good with children. Arnie had been great with kids. Had been over the moon about the pregnancy.

But look how quickly he had turned his back when it had come to the crunch.

'You've won a heart there,' Don commented as Valentino rejoined them on the deck.

Valentino shrugged. 'I have ten nieces and five nephews back home. Children like to dance in any language, I think.'

'That they do,' Don agreed.

'Actually, sir,' Valentino said. 'I'm glad you're both here.' He looked at Paige, who frowned at him. 'My cousin Alessandro tells me its tradition here to ask, permission of the woman's parents to marry her. So—'

'What?' Paige stood up, effectively cutting Valentino off. Had he gone mad? 'I'm not marrying you, Valentino. I told you that yesterday.'

Valentino reached into his pocket and pulled out a velvet box. He opened it and placed it on the table in front of her.

Paige blinked. The simple square-cut diamond nestled in the satin and dazzled in the direct sunlight. It was simple and beautiful and perfect. Every woman's idea of an engagement ring right there before her. And she wanted to put it on her finger so badly it itched. Instead, she reached down and pushed the lid shut.

'I said no.'

Don and Adele looked at the box and then at each other. 'It's pretty traditional to have the woman's consent first,' Don joked, and Adele dug him in the ribs with her elbow as she fought a smile, mashing her lips together hard.

'Which he doesn't have,' Paige said adamantly.

'Paige, I can't allow our baby to be born outside marriage.'

Paige felt the air around her evaporate. 'Valentino!'

Valentino frowned as Adele gasped and turned to Paige. 'Baby?' she demanded.

Valentino raked his hand through his hair. She had said she was going to tell them. 'You haven't told them about the baby?'

Paige shut her eyes and slowly sat down. 'No,' she said, utterly defeated. 'Not yet.'

Adele looked at Don. 'That explains the appetite.' She turned to her daughter and gave her hand a squeeze. 'Are you okay, darling?'

Valentino could see the worry in their eyes as Paige's parents looked at her with concern. They were no doubt apprehensive about their daughter going into premature labour again.

'A little shocked actually, Mum. And ravenous.'

'Maybe that's a good sign?' Adele suggested. 'You couldn't keep anything down with the twins.'

That was true. She'd actually landed in hospital on a drip twice. 'Maybe.' Paige nodded. But the truth was she was still scared witless about the pregnancy. And she didn't have to look at her parents to know they were too.

Valentino observed the byplay intently. He could see the prospect of a second pregnancy for Paige didn't just affect her and him. That her parents had been a major support for Paige and they were understandably concerned.

'I'm not going to let anything happen to Paige or the baby. You have my word.'

Adele gave a sad smile and squeezed her daughter's hand again. 'I believe you. But for now I think we'd better leave you both alone to talk this through. We'll take McKenzie out to the park.'

Paige nodded. 'Thanks.'

Paige's parents rose and Don held out his hand to Valentino. 'It was nice meeting you. And I appreciate that you want to do the right thing by our daughter.' He dropped his hand after a brief shake. 'It's been a tough few years for all of us. It hasn't been easy as a father to watch Paige go through what she's been through. I trust you understand our less than enthusiastic response.'

Valentino nodded. 'Of course.'

Paige was grateful that Valentino waited till they had all departed before he spoke again. 'I'm sorry. I didn't know your parents were going to be here this morning.'

Paige picked up the velvet box and held it out. 'That didn't seem to stop you.'

Valentino ignored it. 'I'm serious about this, *bella*.'

'So am I.'

'You are carrying my child. It's the honourable thing to do. My duty. My mother would disown me if I didn't do the right thing.'

Duty and honour. Two things that Arnie hadn't been big on. Still, they weren't the words a girl wanted to hear when talking marriage. Arnie had said he loved her and couldn't live without her.

That had worked a treat.

Fortunately she was somewhat more evolved now, her heart hardened to flattery. But there was no way she was making the biggest commitment of her life based on anything other than love. And as she'd vowed to never be so stupid again, she just didn't see how it could work.

Paige placed the box back on the table. 'Listen to yourself. This shouldn't be about what's honourable. About duty. This is a long-term commitment. You are not a long-term guy.'

'I am now.'

Paige gave him a reproving look. 'Are you telling me that the first time you laid eyes on me you knew I was the girl you wanted to marry?'

Valentino didn't think it wise to tell her exactly what he had been thinking that day at the wedding. Suffice to say it had come to fruition a few hours later. 'Love at first sight is not a sound basis for marriage.'

'Maybe not, but it's a good place to start. What about Daniella? Didn't you take one look at her and know?'

Valentino frowned. 'I was twenty-four. I'm pretty sure I wasn't thinking with anything north of my belt. It was lust, not love.'

Maybe it had been lust with Arnie too? Maybe she hadn't fallen in love after all. Maybe his flashy, blond good looks and his total adoration of her had blinded her to the real man beneath.

'And it didn't work out. Neither did you and Arnie.

So maybe approaching marriage like this is the best way to go about it. We don't have to get married straight away, we have time to get to know each other.'

'My mother would say we should have done that first.'

He shrugged. 'So would mine.'

Paige smiled despite her heart pounding in her chest as she prepared to ask the next question. 'Just say I agree to getting married…what happens when you do meet the one and you're trapped in a marriage with me? Do you expect me to be okay with it? Do you expect me to sit back and watch you break our child's heart when you leave me for her? Not to mention McKenzie's heart? Would you fight me for custody?'

'*Il mio dio!* I haven't thought about any of these things.'

Paige tried not to let his avoidance of the answer have an impact on her. 'No kidding!'

Valentino's jaw tightened. 'There will be no other women.'

'What about sex?'

Valentino frowned. 'What about it? I thought you liked having sex with me?'

Paige didn't think her liking it was really the issue. That was a no-brainer. 'If you think I'm going to risk this pregnancy by having sex during it, then you really are crazy.'

Valentino rubbed his forehead. He hadn't thought about that aspect of it. '*No problemo,*' he dismissed.

'You seriously expect me to believe you can go without sex for that long?'

Arnie had cited lack of intimacy as one of the reasons

he was leaving and she'd known their defunct sex life had frustrated him. But she had been exhausted, being at the hospital all day and worried sick about the twins, watching Daisy grow steadily more ill. She'd been emotionally numb and physically disconnected from her body, and sex had been the last thing on her mind.

And, besides, it hadn't felt right, enjoying herself while her children were in Intensive Care, fighting for their lives.

Valentino smiled at her incredulity. He should have been angry with her sexist assumption that he was incapable of going without. But he wasn't. 'You don't think,' he said, his voice dropping an octave as his gaze dropped to the interesting mounds he could now make out beneath her baggy T-shirt, 'I'm imaginative enough to be able to satisfy you in other ways?'

Paige swallowed and to her dismay her nipples hardened in blatant response to his ogling. Her breasts had been sore and tight and uncomfortable but they seemed to flower beneath his gaze.

She was temporarily speechless.

Valentino caught her gaze and chuckled as she folded her arms across her chest. Good, he had her attention. 'I don't want to be excluded from the pregnancy, Paige. I want to be around to feel the baby move and kick, to see your belly grow. To help out when you're not feeling well. To get you ice cream and tomato sauce when you wake up with a craving at three o'clock in the morning. I want to get to know McKenzie as well. I'm going to be in her life too.'

Paige wanted to shut her ears to the cosy picture he

was painting. A flash of McKenzie and Valentino dancing flitted through her mind, the look of adoration on her daughter's face as she'd clung to his neck crystal clear.

How could she expose McKenzie to him, like he was asking? Have her love and adore him when, try as she may, she couldn't believe he was going to stick around.

Especially if something happened to the baby.

Yes, he was telling her he would but he'd spent the last decade of his life constantly moving on from one woman to another. Did he seriously expect her to believe he could reverse what by now must be fairly ingrained behaviour?

'And what if something happens to the baby—?'

'I told you nothing would happen,' he interrupted.

She held up her finger. 'Just go with me here on this, okay? Something happens and I go into labour again at twenty-eight weeks or even less and the baby dies. There's nothing keeping us together after that—there's certainly not love. Are you going to tell me you're going to stick around? Or will you run when it all becomes overwhelming because, trust me…' Her voice wavered. 'It will. What happens to McKenzie then?' Or to her, for that matter. 'It'll be devastating.'

Valentino ran a hand through his hair. 'It won't happen.'

'Goddamn it, Valentino,' she snapped, banging her fist on the table. 'What if it does?'

'You're dealing in a lot of what-ifs.'

'Yeah, well, I have to, I'm her mother, I have to protect her. That's my job.' To say nothing of protecting herself.

Valentino's jaw clenched. 'I make you a solemn promise. I will not walk away.'

'But it would be easier for you to go if we didn't marry. If there was no wedding ring holding you here.'

It was Valentino's turn to slam his hand down on the table in frustration. '*Dio!* Listen to me. I. Will. Not. Walk. Away.' He punctuated each word with a vicious finger stab at the table.

For what it was worth, she believed him. Right now, at this moment, his conviction was palpable. But Paige knew that life cold throw you curve balls and things could change in a heartbeat.

She also knew this was getting them nowhere. They needed a compromise, something to break the stalemate. 'You want to get to know me? Us? Then let's just do that for now. I'm not going to stop you from being involved in the pregnancy, Valentino. I will include you as much as possible.' She picked up the box again. 'Let's spend some time together first and then...' she pushed it across the table to him '...we'll see.'

Valentino picked up the box. Paige looked conciliatory and certainly a lot less exasperated. It was a good compromise. She was so skittish, so hurt from her ex, he suspected if he pushed too much she'd never agree. Maybe he'd have to play it cool for a bit. Prove to her he could be the man she needed him to be.

'So it's not a no? It's a maybe later.'

Paige nodded, even though she knew deep in her heart she would never marry again. 'That's right.'

Valentino examined the box for a few moments and then put it back in his pocket. 'I'm going to keep asking.'

And she was going to keep saying no. She smiled at him. 'I wouldn't expect anything less.'

CHAPTER EIGHT

AND he did. At the end of every week together he asked her again. And at the end of every week she said no. Then they started all over again.

They fell into a routine. He came for tea one night a week after McKenzie was in bed. Paige insisted they wait till her daughter was asleep. She knew how easily McKenzie loved people and she didn't want her becoming too attached.

On Sunday mornings he joined the whole family for breakfast. It seemed less intimate with her parents there as a buffer to his charisma and charm and Paige had to admit she looked forward to it. If for nothing else than to taste what amazing culinary offering he brought with him.

And, of course, they saw each other at work three days a week. Although Paige and Valentino were scrupulous about keeping it strictly professional. No one in the department had an inkling of their private affairs, which was exactly what she wanted.

Paige had also insisted that they tell no one about the baby, including McKenzie, not until she'd passed the twenty-eight-week mark at least. To her surprise, Valentino agreed. As he had with the McKenzie-in-bed rule. It seemed he didn't want to do anything to upset her.

He treated her with kid gloves. Was attentive and sweet. He fed her tempting, delicious creations at every opportunity and made her laugh. Apart from his weekly proposal he didn't push her into any decisions or even try to make a pass at her, despite how alarmingly she wanted to feel his lips on hers again.

It was an urge that grew with each week of pregnancy into an almost unbearable craving. Forget ice cream with tomato sauce! Her hormones went into overdrive as she entered the second trimester and Valentino looked more and more edible.

But he seemed immune to her vibes. It was like he'd decided her body was a temple for his baby and that she was no longer a woman that he'd kissed and made very thorough love to on two very long nights. She was a mother now. A sacred vessel.

She should have appreciated it. And she did. By and large. But sometimes she just wanted to grab him and smack a kiss on that full sexy mouth so badly she could barely see straight.

When she started to feel the baby move at 16 weeks he came over twice a week for tea and spent all day Sunday with them. Which was harder on the raging libido but involved him more, for which he was very grateful.

And Paige really kept him as involved as possible without them actually living under the same roof. He attended the weekly ultrasounds and all the doctor's appointments. When it came to discussing the best course of action to prevent another premature labour, she involved him in all the decisions and even looked to him for advice.

Dr Erica de Jongh, the obstetrician, was confident that although Paige was at an increased risk of having a second premature labour, it was highly unlikely she would this time round because the risks factors from her first pregnancy did not exist in this one.

For a start, there was only one baby and from the weekly ultrasounds they could see their baby boy was growing normally, unlike Daisy who had always been small for dates and suffered from borderline intra-uterine growth retardation.

Erica saw no reason for intervention, fully confident that Paige would go to full term. It was only the patients who went into premature labour for no apparent reason that she tended to treat more aggressively in subsequent pregnancies.

And even though it was true that Paige would never be entirely relaxed, both she and Valentino had confidence in Erica, who specialised in high-risk pregnancies and were happy with her care and her treatment plan. And each week as their little boy grew and did all the right things and there were no signs of trouble, they were more and more encouraged.

The day she turned twenty-two weeks Paige was joined by Valentino in the scrub room as she was nearing the end of her three-minute hand wash. It was their first case of the day.

'So,' Valentino said, wetting his arms and applying the liquid surgical scrub, 'twenty-two weeks today.'

Paige could see the smile in his eyes and knew his dimples would be dazzling beneath his mask. Still, they'd agreed not to talk about it at work. 'Not here,' she murmured.

Valentino chuckled. 'I'm just making conversation.'

Paige rolled her eyes at him. 'It's a nice day is conversation. We need more rain is conversation.'

'Ah.' Valentino shrugged, his arms soaped to his elbows. 'Blame it on my command of the English language. Subtleties are harder to pick up on.'

Paige laughed. Valentino spoke perfect English. He certainly understood subtleties and nuance just fine. 'Poor Valentino.'

As she ran her hands under the water for one last rinse the baby kicked her hard and high as if he objected to Paige teasing his father. She gasped, the motion of her hands freezing as her breath was momentarily stolen by the strength and suddenness of it. She leaned over a little, her hands still elevated above the sink.

Valentino frowned, his hands also ceasing their activity. 'Paige? Are you all right?'

Paige nodded as the baby continued to tap-dance in her womb. 'I think this baby's going to play soccer for Italy.'

Valentino grinned. 'It kicked?'

'Oh, yeah. I think he's awake and ready to party.'

It took Valentino all of two seconds to decide his next

course of action. He abandoned his scrub and reached for her belly, soaped arms and all.

'Valentino!' Paige gasped as his hands made wet imprints on her blue scrubs. She looked over her shoulder. 'They're expecting us inside.'

He ignored her. 'Where?' he asked, shifting his hands around, waiting for the tell-tale movement beneath his palm, desperate to be part of this moment with her. He would never tire of feeling his son move. Her scrubs were an annoying barrier and he ran his hands under the hem until his soapy fingers touched bare belly.

Paige gasped again, quieter this time, her teeth sinking into her bottom lip as she concentrated on keeping her arms sterile and remaining upright while his asexual touch spread sticky tentacles to places lower. Much lower.

He'd felt her belly before. But never skin to skin, always through her clothes. His warm, slippery hands were completely methodical and thorough as he slid them all over her small bump, searching for movement. It was crazy. There was nothing intimate about it at all and yet her nipples hardened and rubbed painfully against the fabric of her bra.

'Valentino…' Even to her own ears it sounded husky and aching. Not that he seemed to be listening, intent on awaiting the baby's next move.

She was about to give him the whole this-is-entirely-inappropriate spiel but then the baby kicked again, another hard jab, right where Valentino's hand was, and he laughed, looking up at her with joy in his eyes, and she forgot about what was appropriate. He turned a few more loops for Valentino's benefit and Paige watched his downcast head, his dark hair visible beneath the semi-transparent fabric of his theatre hat.

'This is just the best feeling in the world, isn't it?' Valentino asked, looking up at her.

Paige smiled and nodded. It was hard not to be infected by his enthusiasm. Even though she could only see his eyes, his joy and excitement were plain to see. He held on for another minute, rubbing his hands around the rise of her abdomen.

Paige, her arms having practically drip-dried by now, shifted slightly. 'I think the show's over.'

Valentino's gaze returned to hers. Her grey eyes had gone all smoky and he became very aware that he was touching her quite intimately. Still, the ripe swell of her felt good beneath his hands. Sexy. Right. He hadn't touched her bare stomach since the night they'd conceived his son and he suddenly realised he missed touching her.

He'd spent so much time trying to distance himself from Paige as a woman that he'd forgotten how good her skin felt. He withdrew his hands as if he was back in fifth grade, being rapped over the knuckles by the nuns.

'Sorry.'

Paige wobbled as his hands left her belly and she ground her clogged feet into the floor to stop herself from pitching forward. She tugged a deep breath into her lungs and nodded at his hands. 'You'd better start again.' Then she flapped her arms to dispel the last drips from her elbows and headed for the theatre doors.

* * *

That Sunday Valentino accompanied McKenzie and Paige to the riverside markets and then they met Adele and Don for brunch at South Bank. It had been months since McKenzie had come down with a sniff or a fever and Paige, at the urging of her parents, had decided to risk an outdoors expedition.

And she was pleased she had. The weather was glorious and McKenzie had been in absolute heaven. She'd worn her external device but, unused to crowds, the background chatter combined with the cool river breeze played havoc with the sensitive external microphone and overwhelmed her quickly. Paige removed it after the first ten minutes and she was much happier.

McKenzie had come along in leaps and bounds with her language skills over the last few months and it was a joy to watch her grow and develop now sound and speech were a part of her world.

It was midday as they got up to leave, passing the lunch crowd on their way out. Paige was feeling quite weary from all the walking around and couldn't wait to collapse on her lounge and veg out for the afternoon.

McKenzie tugged on her sleeve and Paige looked down. Her daughter was pointing at the large, white modern Ferris wheel that was a smaller version of the London Eye and could be seen from all over South Bank. Paige groaned. She'd forgotten she'd promised McKenzie a ride.

'We'll take her,' Adele said, giving her daughter's

arms a squeeze. 'Valentino, drive her home. She looks exhausted.'

Paige felt torn. 'Are you sure?'

'Of course,' Don assured her.

Paige reluctantly agreed and watched her daughter skip off quite happily with her parents. Then Valentino whisked her away and had her ensconced on her lounge within twenty minutes, including a quick stop at his favourite deli.

'Mmm, that feels good,' Paige groaned as she slipped her shoes off and lay down on the squishy leather.

Valentino smiled at the pleasure in her voice, which he could hear all the way from the kitchen. He arranged a fat slice of tiramisu on a plate and picked it up, along with two forks.

'This is just as good,' he announced as he carried it into the lounge.

He lowered himself onto the edge of the coffee table closest to her head, immediately noticing the way her hand rested low on her belly, emphasising her bump. His baby was just there and he was surprised by the urge to link his hand through hers.

His gaze drifted higher and was drawn to the way her shirt pulled taut across her chest. Her belly wasn't the only thing that was burgeoning—her breasts seemed determined to keep pace.

He swallowed. Up until he'd laid his hands on her belly the other day he'd been doing just fine with keeping his distance. Treating Paige as the pregnant mother of his child. Affording her the right amount of reverence and respect. But that smoky look in her eyes had stayed with him and ever since his thoughts had been less than…reverent.

'Tiramisu for two,' he said, dragging his gaze back to her face.

Paige could smell the coffee and chocolate before he even sat down, reviving her somewhat. 'Mmm, smells delicious.'

Valentino passed her a fork and watched as she struggled into a semi-upright position. It was on the tip of his tongue to tell her to stay put, that he'd feed her, but the images that rose to his mind were far from respectful and he feigned interest in the dessert as things shifted and moved interestingly.

He held the plate forward and watched as she attacked the cake with gusto, loading up her fork and stuffing it into her mouth. Her pink tongue lapped at excess cream on her lips and her sigh of bliss went straight to his groin.

'Mrs Agostino is a goddess,' Paige groaned.

Mrs Agostino wasn't alone there. Paige had put on weight and there was a healthy glow to her fuller cheeks. Watching her eat was a divine experience.

She loaded up again and slipped the airy creation into her mouth. She looked at Valentino to share her bliss and noticed he wasn't eating. 'You're not joining me?' she asked, around a mouthful of cake.

Valentino's gaze fell to her mouth decorated in crumbs and cream. *Dio!* Was she trying to kill him?

Paige stilled her chewing and swallowed her

mouthful as the direction of his gaze registered. Her lips tingled beneath the intensity of it. Maybe he wasn't as immune to her as a woman as she'd thought? She felt a surge of feminine hormones power into her bloodstream and arched her back a little. The corresponding rounding of his eyes made the move worth it.

'Valentino?'

Val dragged his gaze away from her breasts. 'Sorry. What? Oh, no, thanks. Here.' He thrust the plate at her. 'You have it.'

Then he shifted off the table and went and sat in the single lounge chair furthest away. It was still a sin to watch her eat but at least he'd removed himself from the temptation of leaning forward and using his tongue as a serviette.

'Mmm, that was amazing,' Paige said a minute later, scraping the last crumbs off the plate before placing it on the coffee table. She should be full but nothing seemed to fill her up these days. She had three years of sparrow appetite to make up for and her stomach was accepting the challenge with gusto.

'Now, if only my feet didn't ache so much, everything would be perfect. Honestly…' she looked at Valentino '…you'd think a theatre nurse would be used to standing.'

Valentino chuckled. 'We walked a lot.' Now she'd stopped eating he felt on a more even keel. He moved across to the end of her lounge. 'Here,' he said, slapping his lap. 'Pass me that moisturising cream. I'll give you a foot massage.'

Paige regarded him for a moment. He looked cool and calm and totally in control again and she wondered if she'd imagined that mad moment when he'd looked at her like she was on the menu. Maybe her hormones were also playing havoc with her eyesight?

Anyway, she wasn't about to pass up a foot rub when her feet were throbbing so she grabbed the cream and handed it to him then shuffled down the lounge till she was almost completely horizontal, her head resting on the arm, and placed her feet in his lap.

Valentino soon discovered there was no such thing as an even keel with her as her heels and her painted red toenails created instantaneous mayhem in his trousers. Praying for strength, he lifted one into his hands and shifted the other to the relative safety of his thigh.

Desperate for something to do other than look at her, he got right on the job, squeezing some cream onto his palms and then smoothing it onto her foot.

'Oh, my God.' Paige's head lolled back against the arm. 'That is so-o-o good,' she groaned as aching muscles responded to his light touch.

Valentino's fingers temporarily forgot their job as her breathy appreciation caused paralysis of everything but the activity in his pants.

'Don't stop,' she groaned, wiggling her toes.

Reaching for sanity, he willed his fingers to continue.

'Maybe you should give up work?' Valentino suggested in a bid to give himself something else to think about other than inching his hand higher up her leg.

Paige lifted her drowsy head. 'Erica seems to think

it's okay to continue. She'll let me know if she thinks I should pack it in.'

'I know. I'm just saying you're exhausted and you're only going to get more tired as the pregnancy progresses.'

'I'm fine,' Paige murmured, her eyes drifting shut as Valentino rubbed her instep and her head lolled back. 'Besides, I can't afford to give up work this early.'

He kept his gaze firmly on her toes with the red nail polish. 'I can support you.'

Paige was too chilled out to be affronted. 'No.'

'Paige—'

Paige smiled at the wounded Italian male pride she heard in his voice. 'No. If I need your help, I'll ask.' She lifted her head from the arm. 'Okay?'

Valentino didn't dare look at her. Her voice was all light and husky—he didn't need to see her looking all loose and relaxed and blissed out. 'Fine.'

'Good,' she murmured, dropping her head back. 'Now, please just keep doing what you're doing.'

So he did. The job would have been a lot easier, however, had Paige remained silent. But every time his fingers strayed to a new part of her foot she gave an appreciative moan and it shot his concentration to pieces. He continued through sheer grit alone and steadfastly refusing to look at anything but her feet and what his fingers were doing.

And not thinking about what they'd like to be doing.

Paige hovered on a blissful plane a few inches off the lounge as Valentino's deep steady strokes soothed all the aches away. She watched him through half-closed lids, diligently concentrating on the job. He hadn't taken his eyes off her feet once. Not even when he'd offered to make her his kept woman.

Anyone would think he was a professional masseur, for crying out loud.

Just looking at his bronzed hands on her pale skin was building a fire deep down low. The deep press of his fingers sent streaks of sensation from her foot up her instep to her inner leg and on to her entire body. She was melting into a puddle of desire, a boneless mass of longing.

It was wrong on so many levels. She'd told him this wasn't going to happen. But she wanted him more at this moment than she ever had.

And he was being Mr Professional.

Paige squirmed her body to ease the ache inside and pressed her palm to her belly for some outside fortification. How was she going to get through the next weeks without jumping his bones?

The squirm was his limit. He'd been fine till she'd moved but things jiggled in his peripheral vision and he couldn't stop himself from turning his head and looking his fill.

Her hand rested on her belly in a pose he'd seen more and more often these last few weeks since her tummy had popped out. Her habit of wearing baggy clothes and her baggy scrubs had allowed her to hide it from others, but he knew. He'd felt it.

He knew.

She was wearing a skirt that was too big, its folds hiding her legs all morning, but lying horizontal the folds fell away and the skirt very neatly outlined thighs that had filled out beautifully over weeks of feeding her the most tempting food he could find.

Paige popped her head up. 'Hey,' she protested quietly. 'You stopped.'

Valentino looked down at his stilled hands, surprised. 'I'm sorry.' His gaze returned to her hand splayed down low on her stomach. He wanted to see it. He wanted to gaze on his child growing inside her. 'Can I…can I look?'

Paige's breath stuck in her throat at his intense gaze. He looked so unsure. Valentino, who always looked so sure of himself. She could have no more refused him than have got her boneless body up off the couch. She locked her gaze with his and slowly inched the fabric of her shirt up her abdomen until she was exposed to his view.

Valentino sucked in a breath at the sight of her small round belly. His child grew there. 'You're beautiful,' he murmured. 'May I?'

Paige nodded and watched as his hands left her feet, slid up the sides of her legs, over hips that were less angular these days and onto her stomach. Her muscles contracted beneath his hands as he pushed the waistband of her skirt down slightly and they moved to cradle his child.

Valentino leaned forward and Paige widened her legs to allow him better access, and when he dropped a string of kisses across the swell of her belly her eyes blurred with tears and her fingers speared into his hair.

His tongue found her skin, laving her belly, and she felt the erotic scrape of his three-day growth deep down inside. When he dipped into her belly button she cried out.

Valentino looked up from his ministrations, his chin resting against the rise of her stomach. Her lips were parted and her smoky eyes glazed. Not taking his eyes off her, his hands moved slowly up, pushing her shirt as they went. When they found the lace-enclosed mounds of her breasts she shut her eyes and arched her back and Valentino swiped his thumbs over the taut peaks of her nipples.

Her whimper was soul-deep satisfying and he wanted to kiss her mouth so badly he was moving before he knew it, rising on his knees, looming over her, dropping his head closer and closer to her moist parted lips.

And when she raised her head to shorten the gap there was no holding back. Her mouth was sweeter than he remembered and the moan deep in her throat as she parted her lips widely, inviting him in, mingled with his.

He couldn't get enough of her mouth. Or the curve of her neck or the sweet spot behind her ear. His hands pushed aside her bra cups and she arched her back, pushing herself harder into his palms.

He dropped his head to suck a taut bud into his mouth and her swift indrawn breath was harsh in the silent room. He released it and looked down into her flushed face, her lips moist and ravaged from his ministrations.

Paige's breath sawed in and out of her lungs as she burnt up beneath his incendiary stare. She wanted him in her so badly she could almost feel him.

But.

'We can't…' Actually, technically, they could. Erica

hadn't forbidden it at all. But Paige didn't want to risk anything.

'I know.' He nuzzled her neck. 'Move over,' he whispered. 'Lie on your side.'

Paige gave him kudos for having a plan. She was beyond such things. But her body knew what it wanted and eagerly followed his instructions. And then they were on their sides facing each other and Valentino's mouth was plundering hers and his hands were roaming over her breasts and stomach and pushing the waistband of her skirt lower, lower, and repeating the process with her underwear.

Her hands had a mind of their own too as they plucked at Valentino's shirt, pulled at it, lifted it over his head. Then reached for the clasp and zipper of his trousers, making them seem flimsy as she quickly undid them. His erection strained against his underwear and she pushed it aside too.

'*Dio!*' Valentino groaned into her neck, and shut his eyes as her hand enclosed him, squeezed him.

'You feel so good,' Paige murmured, milking the length of him.

'So do you,' Valentino gasped, his mouth closing over a dusky nipple as his hand found its way between her legs.

When his mobile rang it took several seconds for either of them to even hear it over the beat of their hearts and the heaving of their breath.

Valentino lifted his head and Paige pulled him back to her. 'Ignore it,' she whispered.

But Valentino had a separate ring for family members

so he knew it was one of his sisters. He did a quick calculation in his head, surprised to find he was capable
and also realising with a sinking feeling it was three in
the morning back home. He knew they wouldn't be
ringing at that time for anything trivial.

He pressed a hard kiss to Paige's mouth and then laid
his forehead against her chest. 'I'm sorry. I have to get
it. It's one of my sisters.'

Paige almost wept when he rolled away from her, adjusting his clothes and fishing in his back pocket for his
mobile. She certainly wasn't capable of movement.
Definitely not capable of fixing her own clothes as her
blood pounded like the ocean through her head and the
room spun merrily around.

Valentino flipped his phone open and turned his back
to her. She looked rumpled, dazed, her mouth glistening, her nipples engorged, her belly round with his child.
He could smell her all around him and she looked thoroughly seduced. The temptation to end the call and turn
his phone off was far too great.

'Ciao.' It was harsher then he'd meant it to come out
but, really, his sisters had always had a sixth sense for
interrupting at very inappropriate moments.

Paige listened absently to the conversation in Italian
she didn't understand. It was brief and something was
obviously wrong as Valentino's voice grew urgent and
his words quickened.

He snapped the phone shut and turned back to her.
Paige was still lying on the lounge, clothes skew, belly
on proud display. She looked utterly sexy and he'd give
anything to rewind time and delay the phone call.

'I'm sorry. That was my sister Carmella.' He raked a hand through his hair. 'My mother has been in a car accident not far from where we live.' He shut his eyes briefly as his sister's hysteria clawed at his gut. 'They're flying her to Rome for exploratory surgery.'

In the face of Valentino's wretchedness the sexual fogged evaporated and Paige pulled herself together. 'Oh, Valentino!' she gasped, climbing off the lounge, yanking her shirt down and adjusting her skirt. 'Is she all right?' she asked as he opened his arms and drew her close.

'I don't know. No one knows anything at the moment. I…have to go.'

Paige felt the blow to her heart immediately. She pushed away from his chest and plastered a resolute look on her face. 'Of course you must. Go. Go now.'

Valentino was torn. He couldn't believe in a few short months a woman had become just as important as his family. 'Come with me.'

Paige blinked. What the…? Had the haze of lust fried his brain cells. 'I…can't. I can't just up and leave. I have McKenzie and work and—'

'It'll just be a few days, maybe a week, until I know. Your parents—'

'No,' she interrupted, dismayed at his lack of understanding. 'I'm not leaving McKenzie.'

Valentino tensed, taken aback by her rejection and struggling to appreciate her reasons. 'Fine.'

'Valentino,' she said, stepping towards him, reaching for him. How had they gone from the heights of sexual dizziness to this? 'You know this isn't possible.'

A nerve jumped in his jaw and he flinched as she touched him. 'Anything's possible.'

Paige dropped her hands from his chest. 'No. That's what I've been trying to tell you. You can drop things and just leave. Like right now.' Like he no doubt would for the rest of their lives. Would he want to take their baby too? 'I can't.'

Valentino could feel irrational anger simmer in his blood. He grasped her by the upper arms. 'Marry me.'

Paige could feel the bite of his fingers peripherally only. She knew this was coming from a deep well of concern for his mother but it didn't make it any less difficult to deal with.

If only things were different…

But they weren't.

Paige shifted against the restraining bands of his hands. 'No. Go to your mother. Go home.'

It took a few seconds for her words to sink in and he released her, rubbing at her upper arms, smoothing where he had hurt her. 'I'm sorry,' he said.

Paige linked her arms around his neck and gave him a fierce hug. 'It's okay. Now go.'

Valentino pulled back slightly, slammed a hard kiss against her mouth and then turned away.

It wasn't until she heard the front door shut that Paige realised the awful truth. She loved him. Loved a man who didn't love her back. And there was nothing she could do about it but keep it to herself and never let him know.

CHAPTER NINE

Two weeks later Valentino lay horizontal in his business-class seat, wide awake, somewhere over the Pacific Ocean. The lights in the cabin had been turned down low and most sensible travellers were using it to grab some shut-eye. They'd be landing in Brisbane in just over four hours.

But he couldn't sleep.

He was impatient for the plane to fly faster, to get there sooner. He needed to see Paige. To tell her that he loved her.

It was something he'd known the minute he'd walked out of her door that momentous afternoon and had kept to himself for two weeks. Well, not strictly to himself. He'd told his mother about the baby and she'd demanded to know about Paige. She'd asked him point blank if he loved her and he'd been able to say yes with utter conviction.

But he hadn't been able to confirm Paige's feelings for him to his mother. The truth was he just didn't know how she felt at all. She'd been keeping him at a distance, protecting her damaged heart for the entire time he'd known her. Valentino just didn't know if she'd ever allow herself to fall in love again.

Sure, there was something between them. He knew that. There was a strong physical attraction. He sincerely doubted whether they'd ever be able to keep their hands off each other for any length of time. And there would always be their son.

But he wanted to be more in her life than just the father of their child. A part-time parent. Someone to scratch the itch when it got too much to bear for both of them. He wanted to love and cherish her. Introduce her to his family as his bride. He wanted to grow old with her.

He'd come a long way since his infatuation with Daniella. The young love he'd felt for her was lightweight compared to this heavy feeling in his chest. It had been impulsive and superficial. Skin deep.

What he felt for Paige reached right down to his soul. It was complex, multi-faceted. Messy and complicated. Especially in comparison to the easy, carefree time with Daniella. But maturity was a wonderful thing. He now knew sometimes good things didn't come easily. Sometimes they had to be fought for.

And if that's what it took then he'd do it, because he most certainly knew his life would be empty without her by his side.

Paige rubbed her back absently as she sat in her office chair and updated the charts from the day's surgery. It was hard to concentrate when her mind kept drifting to

Valentino and the fact that in two weeks she'd received three lousy texts.

One had been to say his mother had undergone an emergency splenectomy and was doing well. The next had come four days later to say she was being discharged and he was staying another week or so. And the last a couple of days ago, which had informed her he'd be back soon.

She'd been worried sick about him but he hadn't answered any of her calls or returned any of her messages. He couldn't have been any clearer about her lack of importance to him if he'd opened his mouth and told her.

And it hurt.

Worse than with Arnie. Way worse than with Arnie. Because she'd been an infatuated, blind fool with him but she'd walked into this one with her eyes wide open and the door to her heart firmly shut, but she'd opened the damn thing anyway. Flung it wide open despite her misgivings. And not just her heart but McKenzie's heart too. She was the worst kind of fool.

Another tightening sensation gripped her belly and she had to stop what she was doing and rub at it. She'd been having irregular Braxton-Hicks' contractions on and off all day, no doubt aggravated by standing in a cold theatre in hard clogs.

She'd panicked earlier in the day when the first one had hit in the break between theatre cases and she'd rung her obstetrician in a state of absolute dread, fearing the start of another premature labour.

Not that it felt like it had with the twins at all, just an

occasional tightening, but at only twenty-four weeks and with her history, any little niggle was cause for fright.

After asking succinct questions, Erica had assured her they were Braxton-Hicks' contractions, which were perfectly normal. Not having had any before her first pregnancy had come to a rather early finish, Paige was ignorant to what they felt like, although she'd heard pregnant women and mothers talking about them frequently.

Erica had talked her through the things to watch out for and by the time Paige had hung up the panic had receded and she'd got a grip. Braxton-Hicks were a perfectly normal sign of a perfectly normal pregnancy. They were a good thing. She was going to have a normal pregnancy and deliver at a normal time.

She picked up the pen and starting writing again.

'Paige?'

Her hand stilled in mid-word and her heart contracted as her gaze flew to the doorway. Valentino stood there, taking up all the space, looking as sexy as ever in a haggard twenty-four-hour-flight kind of way. Rumpled clothes, jaw heavy with stubble, bleary eyes and unruly hair.

Actually, he looked like hell.

Good.

She stifled the urge to get up and run to him. No matter how her arms ached to hold him and her heart bled, she would not debase herself with him any more. He'd made it perfectly clear where she stood.

'Valentino,' she murmured, her fingers strangling the pen. Another Braxton-Hicks came and she frowned as it gripped her belly hard, much closer and stronger than any of the others. How long had it been since the last? 'How is your mother?'

Valentino saw the wariness in her eyes. The frigid coolness of them. It hadn't been the welcome he'd expected. Not that he'd known what to expect but the way they'd left things he'd hoped for a little more warmth. Maybe even pleasure lighting those expressive grey pools.

Her shuttered look certainly wasn't conducive to confessing his undying love. 'Fighting fit again. Not much keeps her down for long.'

Paige nodded, her jaw cramped with the effort of keeping her voice evenly modulated. 'Good to know. I'm pleased she came through it well. It must have been worrying for all of you.'

Valentino frowned at her formality. He didn't want this. He wanted to sweep her up and lay her down, see how much her belly had grown in the interminable two weeks he'd been away. Kiss it. Kiss her. Tell her how much he loved her. 'Is everything okay?'

Her shoulders tensed. 'Fine.'

Valentino walked into her office and stood in front of her desk, hands on his hips. He was so tired. All he wanted to do was lie down with her, fall asleep with his hand on her belly. 'You seem…upset.'

A bubble of rage combined with another sharp pain spurred her into standing. She was so angry with him the Braxton-Hicks was secondary. Was he seriously that obtuse? 'Upset? Why on earth would I be upset?' she snapped. 'You don't answer your phone or return my calls. You could have plunged into the ocean days ago for all I knew.'

Paige hated how she sounded. Like a spurned lover, or, in his case, a discarded girlfriend. But she couldn't stop as the pain gripping her belly increased in length and intensity.

She glared at him. 'I was worried sick about you.'

Valentino was unsure whether it was a good thing or a bad thing that she was mad. She'd been worried about him? Did it mean she cared? 'I texted you.'

Paige slammed her hand against the desk. 'Three times! Three lousy times in two weeks? You profess to want to marry me, for us to be a family together, yet you can't even ring me when you get there to tell me everything's okay? You text me?'

Valentino blinked, taken aback by her fervour. It was true he hadn't rung. But that had been deliberate. He'd known that the minute he heard her voice he would have told her he loved her and he hadn't wanted that for her. Not over the phone.

He'd wanted to say the words face to face. So, no, he hadn't rung. But he'd dialled her number a hundred times and listened to her messages over and over again, wishing she was by his side.

And then there was the other side of it. If he'd told her he'd loved her and she'd rejected him or, worse, panicked and run, he would have been a half a world away, unable to do anything about it. At least face to face she couldn't run or hide.

'Nothing to say?' she snapped. 'Damn it, Valentino,

I—' Paige broke off as another pain assailed her down low, doubling her over. She gripped the desk with both hands.

Valentino rushed to her. 'Paige!'

Something was wrong. 'Help,' she cried, clutching Valentino's sleeve. That hadn't felt like a normal, natural Braxton-Hicks. That had felt exactly like it had with the twins when her membranes had ruptured at twenty-eight weeks and she'd been eight centimetres dilated. Exactly.

'I think I'm in labour.' And she burst into tears.

Valentino stared at the top of her downcast head, his arm going around her back, supporting her against him.

No.

No, this could not possibly be happening. He'd told her it wouldn't. He'd told her he'd look after her.

Paige turned a tear-streaked face to him. 'I'm only twenty-four weeks. We have to stop it.' She grabbed the front of his shirt. 'We have to.'

Valentino fought a tidal wave of emotions. The woman he loved was in distress, fighting pain and a bunch of demons. And his baby, his son, possibly also in distress, was too young to survive.

But he couldn't afford to let the wave sweep him up and carry him out to sea. She needed him. So did his son.

'We will,' he said, grim determination in his eyes as he swept her up into his arms.

'What are you doing?' she cried.

'Taking you to A and E. I'll call Erica to meet us there.'

Valentino's long strides took them quickly through the lounge and he deposited her gently into the wheel-chair they always kept in the department. Paige's anguish tore at his gut but he blanked it out as he pushed her to the lifts, using his mobile to call Erica.

'Have your membranes ruptured?' Valentino asked.

'No,' Paige wailed.

He relayed it to Erica, listened for another moment and then snapped his phone shut. Another contraction hit as they entered the lift and Paige cried harder, reaching back for his hand. 'Its okay, Paige, just breathe. Erica's ten minutes away.'

The ride in the lift was the longest of his life and by the time he wheeled Paige into St Auburn's chaotic accident department he was running on sheer adrenaline.

Nat was the first person they saw. Her initial look of welcome quickly turned to alarm as she took in the situation. She knelt beside the wheelchair. 'Paige! Whatever is wrong?'

Valentino answered for her. 'She's twenty-four weeks pregnant and having contractions.'

Nat blinked. 'Pregnant?'

'Yes,' Valentino snapped. 'Pregnant. Erica de Jongh is on her way.'

Natalie didn't need any more information. She didn't reprimand her friend for lying to her on the phone all those months ago when she had rung to check on her. In thirty seconds a blubbering Paige was in a cubicle and being transferred onto a gurney.

'I'll just get the CTG,' Nat said, ducking out of the curtains.

Paige, who was lying on her side, her back to Valentino, had curled herself into a ball and was sobbing quietly. Valentino couldn't bear to see it. 'Paige,' he murmured, placing his hand on her shoulder and applying gentle pressure to get her to face him.

'Go away,' she choked out, giving her shoulder a violent shrug. 'Just go away, Valentino. It'll save you the effort later.'

Her anguished insult hit him square in the solar plexus. 'I'm not going anywhere,' he said, pulling at her shoulder again.

Paige felt a block of rage like molten rock wedge in her chest as she flung herself back to face him. 'I told you. I told you this would happen again and that I didn't want to get close to another baby, to love another baby.'

She half sat, wiping at her streaming eyes and nose. 'But, no, you said it'd be fine, you said it wouldn't happen. You...' she poked him viciously in the chest '...made me go along with it. You...' another poke '...made me want him.'

Valentino's heart broke at her torment. 'Paige, we don't know what this is yet.'

Paige shook her head violently. 'I do.' She knew deep in her bones. 'I. Do.'

Valentino tried to take her hand but she snatched hers away. 'We discussed this contingency with Erica—'

A contraction gripped her and Paige's gasp interrupted him. She tried to breathe but was crying too hard at the same time. It eventually eased and then Nat came in with the CTG machine and hooked the belt around her bump. She squeezed Paige's hand. 'Erica will be here really soon.'

Paige watched the curtains fall back into place as Nat left. She looked at Valentino, so strong and positive, and felt weary, old beyond her years. 'I can't do this again, Valentino.' Paige heaved in deep breaths. 'Do you hear me? I can't do it. I don't have enough strength for this.'

'Yes, you do, Paige. You are the strongest woman I know.' He brushed at her fringe. Her face was all red and blotchy, her nose and eyes were streaming and he cupped her cheek, using his thumb to wipe at her tears. 'Look what you've been through already. Look how you survived. You're a survivor.'

Paige angled her head and leaned her face into his palm and shut her eyes, two more tears squeezing out and trekking down her face. 'Why can't something just go my way for once?' She opened her eyes and straightened her head. 'You told me it would be okay,' she whispered. 'I trusted you.'

He placed his other hand on her face so he was cupping both cheeks. 'You can trust me. I'm not going to let anything happen. We'll get an ultrasound and if it is preterm labour then you'll go on nifedipine and the labour is going to stop and you're giving up work and going on bed rest and I'm going to support you and feed you and pamper you and this baby will go to full term and then we're getting married because I love you and we're going to Italy for a honeymoon and we're taking the kids.'

Paige was feeling so churned up she found it difficult to follow his stream-of-consciousness speech. She wasn't even sure if she heard him right. But the conviction in his words was strong and she so wanted to believe him.

And had he actually said the L word? She sniffed and said, 'What?'

Then the curtains snapped back and Erica arrived, pushing a portable ultrasound machine and looking calm and efficient and in control. Valentino squeezed her hand and they and their future faded away as the immediate danger to their baby took precedence.

'How are you doing?' she asked both of them as she switched on the machine and fiddled with some dials.

'Lousy,' Paige admitted.

Erica nodded. 'You?' she asked Valentino.

'Scared witless.'

Paige looked at him, startled. He hadn't seemed in the least bit afraid. He'd been commanding and confident and had got her to A and E and arranged for Erica to be here and told her everything was going to be okay. He'd been the epitome of cool, calm and collected, especially in the face of her histrionics.

Erica nodded again. 'Normal, then.' She inspected the graph readout the CTG had traced.

Her face gave nothing away but that just made Paige even more frantic. 'It's bad, isn't it?'

Erica looked her in the eye. 'It's showing regular strong contractions. But the baby's heart rate is steady and there are no decelerations. He doesn't appear to be in any distress. Let's have a look first, okay?' She placed a condom over the trans-vaginal probe and squirted warmed lubricant on it.

Paige grabbed Erica's sleeve. 'Please tell me it's going to be okay.'

Erica glanced at Valentino then back to Paige. She shook her head. 'I don't know yet, Paige. But I will in a second. Let's be sure, okay?'

Paige felt a hot tear escape out the corner of one eye and tried not to tense as she drew her knees up and Erica inserted the probe beneath the sheet. Valentino squeezed her hand and dropped a kiss on her shoulder, which made her tear up even more.

An image flickered on the screen and she shut her eyes tight, turning her head into Valentino's shoulder. She couldn't bear to watch.

After what seemed like minutes Paige couldn't take the silence any longer, convinced Erica was trying to find a way to tell her she was almost fully dilated again. She glared at Erica. 'Well?'

Erica flicked a switch and the sure and steady beat of their baby's heart filled the cubicle. Paige broke down at the glorious sound. It seemed so strong but Paige knew at twenty-four weeks their son was so very, very fragile. Too young to be in the outside world.

Erica removed the probe and switched off the machine. She looked at Valentino, his arm around Paige, who was weeping quietly. 'The good news is you haven't dilated at all.'

Paige clutched at Valentino's sleeve as the news sank in. He kissed her head and for the first time since she'd realised she was in labour, Paige felt a ray of hope.

'But. You are fifty per cent effaced.'

Valentino knew both effacement—shortening and thinning of the cervix—and dilatation were required for the baby to be delivered. 'So, it's definitely preterm labour?'

Erica nodded. 'I'm afraid so.'

Paige was incapable of anything as she went from fragile hope to the walls crashing around her. It was happening all over again. She was going to give birth to Val's baby soon. Too soon. A hundred memories of Daisy and McKenzie when they had first been born floated before her.

And her son was going to be even earlier. A whole four weeks of crucial development time.

'So what's the plan?' Valentino asked.

'Oral nifedipine regime to relax the uterus and hopefully stop the contractions, even if it's only for a few days to give us time to administer some steroids to mature the baby's lungs.'

Valentino nodded. 'And then?'

'Hospital for a few days, monitoring blood pressure and regular ultrasounds to check on the cervix.'

He nodded again. Nifedipine's normal use was as an anti-hypertensive and had only been used regularly in an obstetric drug in relatively recent times. Paige's blood pressure would need close monitoring. 'And then?'

'If we can stop the contractions, home on twice-daily tablets and lots of bed rest. If she makes it to thirty-six weeks we take her off the medication and let nature take its course.'

Valentino's methodical medical mind prioritised and

sorted. 'So, the worst-case scenario is that we buy a few days. The best case is we go to term?'

Erica nodded. 'Spot on.'

Paige was taking none of it in. She was numb now. Numb all over. There were no more tears left. Flashes of three years ago bombarded her—the twins on life support, Daisy's tiny white coffin, Arnie walking away—as she tried to reach a mental place where she could shut down her emotions and deal with the next few days, maybe months if Valentino's child was a fighter.

Juggling McKenzie and watching Valentino become ever more distant.

A sob caught in her throat.

'Paige!'

Valentino's voice invaded her thoughts and the mental place moved further out of reach. She looked at him as if seeing him for the first time.

'Leave me alone,' she whispered.

Valentino could see her withdrawing before his eyes and he wanted to shake her. *Dio!* He would not let her give up. This wasn't a battle he could fight on his own, neither could his son. She had to believe it was going to be okay too. 'No.'

Paige had started to recede again and his insistent denial dragged her back. 'What?'

'I said no.'

Paige shook her head. He truly didn't understand how much of her had died inside her last time. 'Just do what needs to be done,' she muttered. He said he loved her? Then he could do that for her.

Valentino looked hopelessly at Erica. 'What do I do?'

Erica gave him a grave smile. 'What she asked you to do. Do what needs to be done.'

Valentino glanced at Paige, so near and yet so far. 'Okay, then.'

Paige swallowed pills and lay passively as they put in an IV and gave her a steroid shot and took her blood pressure endlessly. She didn't feel the belt of the CTG strapped to her abdomen or notice the contractions slowing and then stopping or Valentino's bedside vigil when she was finally transferred to Maternity.

Inside her head she was in a warm dark place with her babies—McKenzie and Daisy and her little boy—and she was singing them a lullaby and as she drifted to sleep they were all happy.

Two hours later Erica strode into Paige's room to check on her patient. She headed straight to the constant readout on the graph paper. 'They've stopped,' she murmured.

Valentino nodded, too exhausted from his flight, which seemed a million years ago now, and worry about Page's mental state to truly appreciate the deep well of joy and sheer relief of his son being okay.

They'd dodged a bullet.

Erica looked down at him and gave his shoulder a squeeze. 'She'll be all right,' she murmured. 'Paige has been through a lot. It's just her way of coping. She'll be a different person when she wakes.'

Valentino nodded but his heart felt heavy as Erica

left. He'd been so excited about the baby—his son. About becoming a father. About the things they'd do together. He truly hadn't considered the mental implications for Paige. She'd tried to tell him she couldn't cope with another poor outcome and he'd swept all her objections aside, promising her hearts and rainbows.

He'd been an arrogant man.

'I'm sorry,' he whispered at her sleeping profile, looking still and pale in her white hospital gown against the white hospital sheets.

He'd been so wrapped up in being in love with her and their joyful future he'd forgotten how truly badly love could hurt.

Paige's arm slipped off the bed and she jolted awake with a gasp. Valentino jolted awake too. 'What is it? Are you okay?' he asked, lifting his head off the bed where it had fallen an hour ago. He stood and loomed over her, blinking bleary eyes and fighting a thick fog of fatigue.

Paige took in the room and the drip and tried to remember what had happened. Her mouth was dry and she had a headache. She looked at him with frightened eyes. 'The baby?' Had they taken the baby?

She reached for her belly, expecting flatness and to feel pain from an incision.

'It's okay,' Valentino soothed, placing his hand on top of hers. 'He's still there. Feel him,' he urged, running the flat of her hand around her bump. 'Erica managed to stop the contractions.'

He pushed aside the bedside chair and checked the nearby growing pile of graph paper. 'Nothing,' he said. 'Not one single contraction.'

Paige's heart banged in her chest. Dared she even hope he was telling the truth? 'Really?'

Valentino smiled. 'Really.'

'So…it's going to be okay?'

'Erica's encouraged by your uterus's rapid response to the medication. You'll need to stay on it but…'

Paige couldn't believe what she was hearing. The last thing she remembered she'd been preparing herself for the worst. 'I'll take a truckload of the stuff if that's what it takes.'

Valentino chuckled for the first time since he'd landed. 'Two a day should be enough.'

Paige laughed as Valentino resumed his chair. His chin rested on his hands and he looked utterly exhausted. His stubble was longer still and his clothes more rumpled. His hair looked as if it had been raked to within an inch of its life. 'You should go home,' she murmured. 'You look totally exhausted.'

Valentino rubbed his chin against the sheets and it rasped into the silence. 'I'm not leaving,' he said. 'I'm never leaving.'

Paige swallowed. She believed him. The man had seen her at her lowest ebb and was still here. Arnie had never been good with her tears and hadn't been able to cope with her grief. He certainly would have been at a loss with her withdrawn state.

Valentino had just taken it in his stride.

'I'm sorry about earlier. I don't know where I went...I totally freaked out.'

Valentino slid his hand back to her rejoin hers nestled against her belly. 'You went where you needed to go. It's okay.'

Paige gave him a small smile and yawned as her eyelids fluttered shut.

'Go to sleep,' he urged. 'I'm staying right here.'

Paige nodded but something niggled at the back of her mind as she drifted off. Three seconds later she was wide awake and sitting bolt upright, her heart in her mouth. 'McKenzie!'

Valentino squeezed her hand. 'She's fine. She's with your parents. I've been giving them regular updates.'

'Really?' she demanded, her pulse still racing.

'Really,' he assured her, reaching his arms up to push gently against her shoulders. 'Go to sleep.'

Paige complied as her heart rate settled and her breathing became deep and even, yet still something niggled.

Paige wasn't sure how much time had elapsed since she'd last woken up but she could see a slight pink hue lightening the sky through a gap in the curtains.

Her gaze drifted to Valentino's sleeping face. For the first time he actually looked his thirty-seven years. A lock of his luscious hair had fallen forward and was kissing his eyelid. It was such an endearing picture her heart filled with her love for him. She forgot all about being mad at him earlier.

What did that matter now? He had been her true hero tonight and she loved him completely.

And suddenly she was able to put a finger on that strange niggly feeling from earlier as memories from yesterday afternoon rushed back. He had told her he loved her too. And today, at the breaking of a new dawn, after a night of miracles, she was going to embrace it and choose to be happy.

Paige advanced her finger slowly and gently lifted the stray lock back into place. He murmured and stirred and then opened his eyes.

She gave him time to focus. 'Good morning,' she whispered.

He licked his dry lips and smiled. *'Buongiorno.'*

She smiled back, her toes curling at his husky morning voice and sexy accent. 'You told me you loved me.'

Valentino stilled for a moment and searched her face. She seemed relaxed. Happy even. 'Yes.'

'Did you mean it?'

'Assolutamente.'

Paige smiled, not needing a translation for that one. 'And when did you have this particular epiphany?'

'About ten seconds after I left your house to go to the airport a fortnight ago.'

Paige laughed this time. 'I think that was about when I had mine.'

Valentino's heart stopped briefly before skipping madly in his chest. He slid his hand to her belly. 'Really?' he murmured.

She nodded, holding his hand close. 'Really.'

'It was before that, though. The moment I fell in love with you. I just didn't realise until much later.'

Paige quirked an eyebrow, intrigued. 'Oh? When?'

'That night at the wedding when you looked so confused as to why out of all the women at Alessandro's wedding I wanted you.'

Paige frowned. 'Why then?'

'Because you truly didn't know how beautiful you were and that, my darling…' he lifted her hand off her stomach and kissed it '…was utterly endearing.'

She could feel her cheeks turn pink. 'I think for me it was when you promised me there would be no sleeping.' Valentino chuckled and she grinned. 'That was a great line. You'll have to teach it to our son when he's older.'

Valentino felt his chest expand. Their son. 'So you're not going to fight me any more? You'll marry me?'

Paige nodded vigorously and snuggled his hand back against the swell of her belly. 'And the four of us will honeymoon in Italy together.'

Valentino grinned. It sounded like bliss. 'I brought this with me from the airport.' He reached into his pocket with his spare hand and pulled out the velvet case he'd produced all those months ago. He presented it to her. 'Will you wear it?'

Paige slipped her hand out of his and flipped open the lid. The diamond glittered beneath the dim overhead light. 'Just try and stop me,' she murmured as she freed it from its satiny cushion and slipped it on. 'See?' She turned it around to show him and he rose slightly and pressed a gentle kiss against her mouth.

'Perfect. Just like you.'

'Just like us,' she whispered. 'Just like him.' And her hand rejoined his as she kissed him back.

EPILOGUE

'HE's perfect. Perfect in every way,' Valentino mused, peeling back the wad of wrapping in the crook of his wife's elbow to reveal his one-hour-old son Ferdinando Lombardi.

Paige smiled as her little boy slept. She couldn't agree more. She was exhausted from a fifteen-hour labour but somehow still too elated to sleep. Erica had taken her off the nifedepine a week ago and their son, after wanting out at such an early stage, had finally decided to make an appearance seven days later, weighing a very healthy three and a half kilos.

'Can we come in?'

Paige looked up to see her parents and McKenzie waiting impatiently in the doorway.

'McKenzie!' Valentino smiled and held out his arms to her.

She rushed into the room. Don and Adele followed at a slightly more sedate pace. Slightly.

Valentino swept McKenzie into his arms and plonked her on the side of the bed. 'Are you ready to meet your little brother?' he said as he signed simultaneously.

McKenzie squirmed with barely suppressed excitement. 'Yes,' she said.

Paige smiled, still in love with her daughter's voice as she turned her son around.

'This is your brother, Ferdinando,' Val murmured, signing as well.

McKenzie looked at him as if he were a baby unicorn she'd found in an enchanted forest, her eyes big and round. 'Nandi,' she said, and leaned forward to kiss the tip of her sleeping brother's nose.

'Looks like he's already acquired a nickname.' Adele beamed, reaching forward to gently touch her grandson's tiny fingers.

Valentino chuckled. 'I like it.'

Paige made way for McKenzie to snuggle into her side and they all gazed on her newborn son's perfection.

'Thank you,' Valentino mouthed after a few moments, interlinking his hand with hers.

'Thank you,' she whispered back.